Hotwife Debauchery

Jenni Winters

Contents

About The Author

Jenni began writing erotica as a way to channel her biggest fantasies. Now, she loves spreading her dirty stories across the web so others can enjoy!

If you LOVE wife watching, cuckolding, cheating wives, and BIG BLACK BULLS, you've come to the right place. Most of Jenni's cuckold stories are based on personal experience, stories of friends, or just her dirty mind in action.

The Hotwife Control Black Lust

Jenni Winters

Chapter 1

Kevin had been annoying me lately. I really needed to put him in his place. Who does he think he is anyways? I swear, sometimes my husband forgets where he stands in our relationship.

For the past few weeks, Kevin had been oddly possessive of me. He kept asking where I am, what I'm doing, and who I'm talking to. How dare he question me like that? It was none of his business. I don't answer to him. He answers to me. In fact, it was his idea that we do this in the first place. I had no idea he would be this clingy.

Kevin had begged me to sleep with other men for the longest time. He finally wore me down. I decided I needed something bigger than his sad excuse of a cock to please me. I needed a real man for some real pleasure.

I enjoyed it so far. I went on a few dates and made out with a few hot guys. However, no one was sporting the large cock I wanted. I became hungrier and hungrier for the one that would really satisfy me.

I walked into the kitchen. Kevin had just finished a beer.

"Hi, Lana. How was your day? Did you meet anyone tonight?"

His questioning really pissed me off. It couldn't be helped though.

"Good. I'm going out tonight. I'm sure I'll be picking up something nice."

Kevin's eyes lit up like a Christmas tree. His jaw nearly hit the floor.

"T-that's nice. W-where are y-you doing?" He asked nervously. I knew his little picker was probably hard imagining another man taking his wife.

"I'm going somewhere nice. I'm going to Light. It's always full of hot and horny men. I'm sure they will all be over me once I walk in."

I was excited about the venue. Light was a new hip night club in the downtown area. And it attracted the darker breed of men. I had talked to my friend, Kara, earlier who suggested I need a big black cock to satisfy my needs.

It turns out; Light is having a big party tonight. I planned on going there and picking out a young, hot stud to take my pussy. Maybe I'd even give Kevin the leftovers if he behaved properly.

"May I come along?" He asked like a little puppy dog.

"No. I want to go alone."

I sat down on the chair and spread my legs apart. I knew Kevin loved to see my pantyhose.

"Will you need me at all tonight?" He asked softly.

I ran my finger across my red hot lips. "I might....if you're a good boy."

I could already spot Kevin's pathetic littlc dick getting hard in his pants.

"I've waited so long for another man to take you." He whispered softly. It was like he had been put into a trance.

Kevin's eyes followed my every movement. It was so easy to control him like a puppet. I spread my legs wider and pulled down my hose to the side. His bulge grew by the second.

My husband began to stroke his cock through his jeans. "Take your hand off that pathetic thing!" I snapped at him. "You seemed to have forgotten that I control that little thing. Stand there while I pleasure myself."

"Yes of course. I'm very sorry, Lana." He said.

"That's right. I bet you want to see a big stud fuck my pussy. Fuck my tight little cunt with his fat cock."

"Oh yes!" Kevin moaned.

I inched my fingers deeper into my pussy. It felt so good. I imagined a black stud penetrating my tight cunt. How wonderful would that feel?

"And do you why do I need such a big cock?"

"Because mine is too small." He whimpered.

"Speak up!" I yelled at him.

"Because mine is too small to please you!" He said loudly.

I laughed. It was true, but sad. "That's right. You're fucking tiny and I need a real man that'll last. You're just a minute man."

"I'm sorry." He said. His face had begun to turn into a nice shade of red.

"I need a big cock to please me. I deserve it, don't you think?" I flicked my bean. It felt so good. My husband's cock couldn't even provide me an ounce of pleasure.

"Yes. You deserve all the cock you can get."

"That's right."

"Do you need help? Please let me give you an orgasm." Kevin begged.

"Stay away. Kneel and watch." I pointed at the ground.

Kevin knelt on the cold marble floor as I rubbed my pussy.

"I'm going to let some young stud fuck my pussy. And guess what? He's going to cum in it. You'd love that, wouldn't you?"

"Yes. I want that so bad, Lana. Please."

"You'll have to lick it clean. I don't want to see a drop after you're done. Got it?"

"Yes. I'll lick it clean."

"That's a good boy."

My fingers slipped in and out at a remarkable pace. Soon enough I reached climax. It felt so good. My inner walls crushed my fingers. It was the best orgasm I've had in months.

"Oh yes! I'm definitely finding a real man tonight." I took my fingers out. They were coated with a thin layer of white sugar.

"Crawl over here, Kevin."

My husband crawled like a dog. "Smell my fingers." I rubbed it right under his nose and pushed his head back. I slapped him a few times for good measure.

"Stay in our bedroom. I'm going out. You need to wait patiently for me."

"Yes of course."

He began walking up the stairs when I stopped him.

"And Kevin..."

"Yes?"

"No jerking off and no cumming. I want you nice and horny for my bull."

"Understood." He replied.

Chapter 2

Light was full of hot and horny men. A saw a big group that eyed me as I walked in. I couldn't blame them. I wore a sexy black cocktail dress that would turn gay guys straight.

The loud music pulsed through my body. I took a seat at the bar as numerous men stared at me from afar. I didn't want to approach them. A real alpha male would approach me. I just had to wait for the right one.

Soon I caught a young black stud checking me out. He looked tall at least a foot taller than me. His muscles were huge as well. I bet he was a NFL linebacker or something. The mystery man couldn't keep his eyes off me. I shifted towards him a little bit so he could get a better look at my tits. I hoped he had a big cock. If he didn't, he would be useless to us.

He smiled big towards me. I reciprocated with a seductive grin. He took the cue and walked on over with confidence. He certainly seemed like an alpha dog.

"Hi." He said. His booming voice penetrated the music in the background. He rested his elbow on the table and slightly flexed his biceps. My pussy trembled in response. He was already more manly than Kevin.

"Hello there." I said calmly.

"Can I buy you a drink?" His deep voice almost seemed hypnotic.

"Of course."

"What's your name?" He said as he called over a bartender.

"I'm Lana."

"Clive." The man replied.

"It's nice to meet you."

"Likewise."

"So...what's a pretty lady like you doing in a place like this?"

"I'm looking for big black cock." I said to him.

Clive chuckled. I guess he didn't expect me to be so frank. "Is that so? Well you've come to the right place."

"Are you sure? Because I need a big cock tonight..." I reached over and tapped his crotch discretely. It felt so big like he was hiding a snake down there. My pussy became wet almost immediately.

"You like?" Clive asked seductively.

"Of course. I want it so bad."

"You want this cock?"

"Yes..."

"Let's skip the drink then. Let's just get down to the fucking."

I smiled at him. I knew Clive was the man for the job. He would really make Kevin jealous. "That sounds lovely." I replied.

Clive took my hand and helped me down from the stool. He escorted me outside the club. Everyone in the crowd seemed to part away like the red sea as we passed. No doubt they didn't want to get in Clive's way.

We called a ride from the valet. Clive grabbed my ass as soon as we sat in the car. I could smell his leathery cologne. It was just so manly. I gave the driver our address so he could punch it into his phone.

Clive immediately ran his fingers down my leg. "I love how smooth they are." He commented.

My nipples became hard like diamonds. Clive reached over and grabbed the back of my head. He pulled me in for a deep kiss. His dark lips covered over mine. They were so warm and soft.

"Mmmm! You're a good kisser." I whispered softly to him.

"You ain't seen nothing yet, lady. I'm going to fuck you silly tonight."

"Oh I can't wait. My husband is going to be so excited.

Hold on a minute."

"Your husband?"

"Yes. He wants to see another man take me." I replied quickly. I reached into my purse and pulled out my phone. This was too good of an opportunity not to tease Kevin.

"I'm going to call my husband. I want you to tell him all the dirty things you're going to do to me."

"And he's okay with all this?" Clive sounded surprised.

"Of course. He wants it even more than I do." I grabbed his crotch before I dialed Kevin. I wanted to feel his big manhood.

"Hello?" Kevin answered the phone before the first ring ended.

"Hello little cuck." I turned on the video feature so he could see our faces. "Guess who I have here."

Kevin's jaw pretty much dropped to the floor. "You found someone?"

"Of course I did."

"I'm going to fuck your wife silly tonight, boy!" Clive took the phone from my hand placed it on the seat next to us. "Enough games. Let's get down to action." He said.

His fingers caressed my panties. His dark, thick fingers played with my clit. Clive reached over and sucked on my nipple.

"Oh! That feels soooooo good, Clive!"

"Clive? Who's that? What's going on over there?" My husband asked frantically. It made me so wet knowing he could hear Clive pleasure me, but he couldn't see a thing.

"Oh Clive! You're so big!" I moaned. The driver looked back at us, but I didn't care. I wanted everyone to know I finally found a big cock to fuck me.

"Kevin are you still there?" I asked as Clive's finger inched deeper into my tight cunt.

"Yes. I'm still here."

"Stay in the bedroom. I'll call you down when we're ready."

I hung up the phone before he could even answer back.

"That was crazy." Clive laughed. He really is your doormat."

"Of course. That's what we agreed to. You see, he's a big shot executive at a fortune 500 company. He bosses people around all day, but the buck ends when he gets home. I control everything."

"Sounds like a fun marriage." Clive smiled.

"It is."

"Now where were we?"

"You were just kissing me." I replied.

Chapter 3

I slammed the front door behind us. I wanted Kevin to hear our dramatic entrance.

"Lana? Is that you?" He yelled from our upstairs bedroom. I could hear the fear and excitement in his voice.

I ignored him. I wanted him to suffer a bit from the teasing. Clive held me close. I loved smelling his cologne. It made me so wet. He leaned in and kissed me. "Oh Clive! You're so big!"

His hardon pressed against my inner thigh. I knew I had picked out the right man for the job.

"Here, sit down." I pushed Clive against the couch. He smiled as I unbuckled his belt and removed his jeans. His briefs contained a huge big black cock. I caressed the material softly.

"Do you want to see it?"

"Yes. I want to see it so bad." I stroked it some more. With every touch his cock seemed to get bigger.

I bent down and kissed the tip softly. "Remove it then."

I pulled his gray briefs off. His cock was so big! I couldn't believe it! It was at least 12 inches long and wider than my wrist. Could something so big even fit in my pussy?

I licked my lips and stroked his big black cock softly. My fingers couldn't even wrap around his manhood.

"Oh my god! It's so big!" I squealed like a pig. "Hold on a second..."

I left Clive dangling at the edge of the sofa. I wanted Kevin to see this so I ran upstairs. He was pacing back and forth in our bedroom.

"Lana! Are you okay?"

"Yes. I'm fine. Are you ready to see me be taken by another man?"

"I'm so excited."

I moved in and grabbed his crotch. "Yes...I can tell. You're going to enjoy this so much. Come down and watch. Clive is going to put your manhood to shame."

I stripped out of my cocktail dress and led him downstairs.

"Well you look even hotter without your clothes on!" Clive remarked. He licked his lips and stroked his large cock for us.

"You see that, Kevin? That's a real cock." Kevin was pretty much speechless. He couldn't believe he was so small compared to Clive.

"Let's see his tiny cock." Clive suggested.

"You heard him, cuck! Strip down." Kevin was a nervous wreck. His hands fumbled around as he stripped down before us.

"Wow! Is that it?" Clive pointed at my husband and laughed his head off.

"Yes, I'm afraid that's all." Kevin's tiny pecker seemed to shrink as we humiliated him.

"Watch how a real man pleases me." I slapped my husband lightly on the cheek.

"You're going to watch me fuck your wife, right?"

"Yes. I'm here to watch." Kevin said obediently. He knew he was in the presence of a superior man.

"And you're going to clean up afterward." I added in.

Clive laughed. "Alright. That's enough foreplay. I want your lips on my cock now."

I quickly knelt before Clive. He was so big. I bent down and my lips caressed his soft head.

"Oh god!" I moaned. Clive grabbed the back of my head and pushed me deeper into his cock. I struggled to take something so big. I could hear Kevin gasp from behind. He was thicker than any man I've ever had before.

My pussy throbbed as I slid my mouth deeper around his shaft.

"Take it!" Clive pushed harder. I groaned as his cock jammed deep down my throat. I gagged on it as the air escaped my lungs.

"Good god!" Kevin moaned.

Eventually, Clive relented his grip on my head. I breathed in air again. The sweet taste of his cock lingered in my mouth.

"Are you okay?" Kevin asked me.

I stared into Clive's dark eyes. He was just so handsome and dreamy. "Never better." I replied.

I straddled him on the couch and we kissed. Our lips locked together as he bit down softly on mine. I grabbed his cock from behind and jerked it softly.

"I want your cock so bad."

"Sit down on the couch." He ordered me. I sat down and held Kevin's small dick in my hand.

"Watch him fuck me. Watch me struggle with his big black

cock." Is squeezed down on his head. Kevin groaned pathetically.

Clive mounted me; his cock rested directly on my clit. He wasn't even in me yet and I moaned like crazy. He pushed his way in as my muscles strained to take him.

"It's so big!" I groaned.

Kevin breathed heavily to my side. I giggled; I could only imagine the thoughts flashing through his little head as a young stud drilled my pussy.

"Oh god! I love your cock!" I groaned

My pussy lips stretched wide to accommodate his monster cock. My clit trembled with pleasure with every single thrust.

I grabbed Kevin's hair from the side. "You could never make me feel like this, Kevin. You're too fucking small."

"I'm sorry." He replied in a deflated attitude.

Kevin's large cock punctured all the way through. My clit rested on the base of his shaft. Soon, the incredible pain was filled with only pleasure.

"Fuck me, Clive! Please!" I screamed. My voice became shrill in a matter of seconds. Throbs of excitement rushed through my body as he rammed in and out of my dirty cunt.

"Yes! Harder! Do it harder!" I begged.

"You are one tight bitch!"

"I know! I need your big black cock!"

Clive turned to my sorry excuse for a husband. "You're pathetic." He grunted in between his thrusts. "You like watching me take your wife?"

"Yes sir." Kevin said in a soft voice.

"That's what I like to hear, cuck!"

Clive pushed up and slammed into my swollen cunt. It was red to the touch. My whole body trembled as our hips smashed into each other like tectonic plates.

Soon, Clive turned me around and fucked me in doggy. I felt the length of his magnificent 12 inch cock against my inner walls.

"Oh god! You are so pathetic Kevin! You could never make me feel like this!" Kevin watched intently as Clive fucked my pussy raw.

"Cum in my pussy!"

"You sure?" Clive asked.

"Yes! Fill me up! I want it now! My husband is going to clean it!"

"Oh yes! I'm going to cum! I'm cumming!"

His cock swelled up and he completely unloaded. I finally came as well. My pussy contracted uncontrollably and squeezed the life out of his fat cock.

Clive managed to thrust one last time as his first wave of cum shot deep into my pussy. The heat spread through my lower stomach.

"Yes! Oh god! More! Fill me!" My head shook from side to side.

Soon after, Clive pulled out and I slumped against the couch.

"Cuck! Come around and clean me!"

Kevin scampered around until he knelt between my legs. "Are you ready?"

"Yes. I've been ready all night long."

"Good. Do it."

Kevin's warm tongue nestled between my pussy lips. Clive had done a good job of coating everything with his white jizz. My husband groaned with pleasure as he sucked another man's cum from my pussy.

I really wanted to tease him so I caressed his cock against my toes. He was so hard. Be blew a load in about 10 seconds. So pathetic! At least he kept cleaning my pussy like a good cuck.

Clive and I made out as Kevin continued to worship our mixed juices. "Clean her good cuck." Clive ordered him.

"Yeah. Make sure it's all clean before we go another round. If you do a good job, I might allow you to suck his cock."

"Yes! Of course!" Kevin said.

His warm tongue continued to clean me out as Clive and I enjoyed our after-sex glow. It was just the beginning of our fun. I never wanted to fuck Kevin's tiny dick again!

Watching Her

Jenni Winters

Chapter 1

Erin and I walked into the resort together. We had enough holiday celebrations with everyone. It was time to just be by ourselves and focus on more important matters. We decided to come to sunny Cancun. It was certainly busy here. A ton of families were all over the place to celebrate the new year.

I pulled my wife in and kissed her softly. "I love you, honey."

"I love you too."

She grabbed my crotch seductively. We checked into our room shortly after. Erin changed into her bikini. I walked behind Erin and held her. It felt nice. My heart beat against her back. I could smell her intoxicating perfume.

My cock hardened against her supple ass. "Mmm, do you want to try and pick someone up?"

"I thought you would never ask, Rick."

Erin turned around and grabbed my hard shaft. Her fingers

crawled up my stomach until she tapped my chin. "You love watching someone else fuck me don't you?"

"Yes..."

"Tell me how much you love it," Her fingers danced around my lips. She teased me with her nails. "Oh I love it so much. I love it when you moan their names."

"Yeah? Well we better find someone quick then..."

"Let's head for the beach bars."

Erin pulled me downstairs. We had done this multiple times before. We had a pretty open marriage. I allowed Erin to sleep with other guys. In fact, I enjoyed watching them fuck her.

It was an incredibly erotic and intimate connection we shared. I trusted her with anything. I knew it was just sex she experienced with these guys and nothing else.

"Perhaps we should try one of those adult resorts," I suggested in the elevator.

"Okay. Let's try asking the front desk?"

"Sure, couldn't hurt."

We made it down to the lobby to ask directions. It was incredibly busy. Karen was manning the front desk still. It was an odd request, but we didn't really care.

"Hey Karen, Erin and I were wondering if you had any recommendations on the best adult resorts around here."

"Well there are a few down the road. I would definitely check out Ambrosia. It's just a few miles down and they're having a big party today."

"Sure, we'll check it out. Thanks for the tip."

Erin and I left for the car. It was a quick drive just like Karen had said. We parked in the garage and couldn't believe what we saw in the lobby.

Everyone was walking around naked and having a huge orgy. There were a few hot couples here. "What do you think, Erin?"

"Wow...when she said it was clothing optional this is not what I had in mind."

"Same.."

"Should we have a look around? Seems like they're having a big party out back."

"Yeah, let's go."

There was a giant courtyard with sand in the back of the hotel. A DJ booth had been set up and a few volleyball courts as well.

It was like one giant party and people were having sex all over the place.

"I think we found the right place," I commented with a giggle.

"Yeah, I'll say. It's pretty crazy."

"Hello there...is this your first time at an orgy like this?"

A handsome man welcomed us in. His ebony skin looked shiny under the sun. He certainly took care of his body. He was ripped and extended his giant hand out to shake mine.

"Hello, I'm Rob."

"Hi, I'm Rick. And this is my beautiful wife, Erin."

"And yes, this is our first time here."

"Really? Well, what are you two into?"

I was a little taken back by the man's bluntness, but I figured we didn't know anyone here so it would be okay to divulge our little secret.

"Well, my wife here loves to fuck other guys and I love to watch."

"Ah you have a hotwife fetish."

"Yes..."

The man smiled. "Well, I would suggest you try our magic glory hole."

"What's that," Erin asked.

"It's just an event we have once a month. We get ten ladies behind a glory hole for an hour and suck off as many guys as possible. The winner gets a free spa treatment. It's very popular around here."

Erin and I looked at each other. We had never done something like this before, but I could tell she wanted to try it.

My wife pulled me aside. "What do you think? It sounds really kinky."

"Sure...only if you want to though."

"Let's do it!" Erin held my hand as we accepted Rob's offer.

"Come with me then. You two are about to have the time of your life."

He led us into the back of the courtyard. There were lots of guys lining up outside already. I had a good look at a few of them. Some of them looked very attractive and this was coming from a straight guy. I wondered if my wife found any of them attractive as well.

Rob led us to the back of the wall where there were separate stalls for the girls. Each one was its own separate room. "Here you are. Whenever you're ready." Rob smiled as he left us alone.

"God...this is so fucking kinky," I remarked.

"I know..." Erin replied. "Should we just go?"

"I don't see any other way."

A big cock was already on the other end. My wife grabbed hold of it and stroked it. I could hear the man on the other end moan.

Erin smiled as she pulled her head down and began sucking on his manhood.

Chapter 2

The man on the other side moaned. "Oh god!"

My wife's tongue rolled around his engorged head. Her lips caressed his skin. I rubbed Erin's clit. She was so fucking wet.

"Oh god! I love your cock"

She sucked on it and shoved it deep into her mouth. The man's cock twitched as my wife pleasured it.

"You're the best cocksucker I've ever had!"

"Why thank you. You're such a gentleman..." my wife nearly blushed.

Erin pulled his cock out of her mouth. She pulled me down and we kissed for a moment. Her warm tongue caressed my lips; it was so soft. My cock hardened as she stroked it a few times. "Come suck his cock for me..."

She didn't need to tell me twice. Erin focused on the head while I focused on his balls. I could feel my wife's saliva drip down. I used it to suck on his balls.

"Oh yes!" The man moaned. He couldn't believe there were two of back there.

Just then Erin had a bright idea pop into your head. "Why don't you come back here and fuck me while I'm sucking someone else!"

"Which stall are you in?"

"Third one from the left."

The man quickly pulled his cock out of the glory hole and rushed towards us. Erin was giddy and I couldn't blame her. The man had an amazing cock.

"Wow...this is so fucking kinky," I whispered to her.

"Yeah I know. You're still into this right?"

"Yeah, of course."

Another mystery man shoved his cock into the hole. My wife

grabbed it and stroked it for a few moments. His cock grew longer.

Just then, the first guy stepped into our booth. It was getting a little crowded in here. "Hello, you're even more beautiful than I imagined."

"Why thank you. I'm Erin. This is my husband, Rick."

"Pleasure to meet you. I'm Antonio."

Antonio wasted no more time with idle chit chat. He was a man of action. He pushed down my wife and pulled her ass up.

"God, you have one sweet pussy."

"Fuck me then. Fuck me hard!"

He pushed his cock into my wife. It was a sight to see. Her cunt was obviously too small. He pushed the first two inches in. His giant head ravaged my wife's cunt. "Oh! Oh!" She groaned.

Erin still sucked on the other man's cock. Her moans penetrated through the thin wooden walls of the booth. I'm sure the other guys on the other side were dazed and confused about what was going on.

"Fuck! Your cock is so big!"

Antonio chuckled as he continued to fuck my wife. He grabbed her hips and rammed his cock into her. It was amazing to watch from the side. I held her hand softly as she took it all.

"Oh god! Yes!" Erin moaned and groaned like a banshee.

She brought the other man to an orgasm. He completely exploded in her mouth and all over her face. "Jesus," I exclaimed!

Eventually she stopped sucking on the other man's cock. Antonio was just giving her too much pleasure. Her cunt was swollen and red. I watched as she bit down on her lip.

Her face was covered in a white frost. I knelt down by her side and looked into her beautiful eyes. She smiled back at me.

I couldn't handle it anymore. I held her cheek with my left hand and we embraced for a kiss. It was so erotic. My cock throbbed. Her tongue licked my lips. I could taste the other man all over her; I didn't mind that at all.

"Mmm!" She moaned into my mouth as Antonio's cock ravaged her cunt.

"Cum in me!"

"Yeah! I'm going to do it," he screamed.

He pumped his cock faster and faster into my wife. Meanwhile, Erin grabbed onto my cock. She jerked it fast like a monkey. I knew I wouldn't last long at this pace.

Antonio and I must have cum at the same time. He exploded inside her cunt while I exploded all over her side.

I closed my eyes and went to heaven. I must have shot at least seven or eight loads onto her side.

"Fuck yeah," Antonio exclaimed. "Thanks for the fuck, sweetheart."

"Thank you," my wife replied.

"Oh god! That was so hot," I whispered to her.

"I know. Come eat me out now..."

Erin smiled as I eagerly lowered my face to her beautiful cunt. It was completely filled with Antonio's cum. "Oh yes! That's the spot Rick!"

I attacked her pussy. My tongue slipped into her folds. His cum was still warm. I lapped it up like my life depended on it. My lips caressed her clit. I sucked on it softly.

Erin wrapped her legs around my head and grabbed onto my hair. "That's it! Keep going!"

My tongue and lips brought her closer and closer to orgasm.

"Fuck yes!"

I felt her inner thighs tighten around my neck. I tasted the mix of her and Antonio's cum. It was absolutely exquisite.

"Fuck! This is the best vacation ever!"

"I know, right?"

Erin and I rested in the booth alone for a few minutes in silence as the chaos of the party continued to erupt around us. It was the most amazing experience we could have ever hoped for on this trip.

Eventually we left. We wobbled out of the adult resort and back to our hotel. Something told me this wouldn't be the last naughty experience on our trip.

Shared With Ebony

Jenni Winters

Chapter 1

I leaned back against the chair outside our pool. A cool summer breeze brushed against my skin as I sipped on a long island ice tea. I watched my husband, Jim, and his old friend, Tyrone, by the grill. The boys haven't seen each other in a few years, but recently reconnected.

As I watched from the distance, I couldn't help but notice the stark physical contrast between the boys. I mean it wasn't just that Jim was your average pale and pasty white guy. Tyrone was just so well built; he obviously kept up at the gym.

My husband had his shirt on, but Tyrone took his off long ago. I admired his jet black skin from the distance. I loved checking out his enormous pecks and his chiseled six-pack. I had to admit, for the longest time I had a big crush on Tyrone.

I've never had a black guy in my life. I grew up in a small white community without any characters of the darker persuasion. For the longest time I've heard my friends rave on about how black men are clearly superior to white guys. Some of my friends swore they had the biggest cocks.

I always fantasized about taking a big black cock in my mouth. I'd love to suck on something so big. After that I imagined that same cock fucking my tight little pussy until I came. It was such a dirty fantasy and no one knew about it even Jim.

The guys seemed to be having a good time. They talked about cars, video games, and all sorts of other things. Meanwhile, I was just enjoying myself at the pool.

"Hey Olivia, can you check my phone for the movie tickets we ordered? I just want to make sure we're all set."

My husband's voice broke my concentration on Tyrone's hunky ebony body. "Sure thing babe." I replied.

I stood up and picked up my husband's phone. He was always such a little nervous nelly. I scrolled through his inbox and found the movie tickets. The boys were still busy talking and grilling the meat, so I decided to peruse the rest of his emails.

A long email chain between Jim and Tyrone caught my eye. I looked up briefly and the boys were still occupied. I took another sip of the cocktail and opened the email.

I couldn't believe what was in it! The email chain started last night, Tyrone's first night with us.

"Dang Jimmy boy! Your wife just gets hotter every time I see her! I want to fuck her silly!"

My loins tingled with pleasure as I saw Tyrone's comment. He wanted to fuck me?

"Well I'm about to fuck her tonight, I'll make sure she screams nice and loud so you can hear her."--My husband wrote back.

I remembered our hot lovemaking session last night. Jim tried everything to get me to moan louder and louder. He even ate my pussy, which he doesn't like to do. Wait...he did it so Tyrone could hear us!

The boys were still busy, so I scrolled through the entire email. The messages even continued after we had sex last night. I couldn't believe the boys were talking about me like this!

"Dang man! I would do anything to fuck your wife."

"Well Olivia's a little bit more conservative man. She probably wouldn't go for that idea."

What?! Did my husband just call me a boring obedient housewife? There was nothing like hearing my dream black man wanted to fuck me silly like a rag doll. My moist pussy tingled with pleasure.

I couldn't contain myself any longer. I brought my knees up so the boys couldn't see. My delicate fingers caressed my wet slit. It felt so good. I imagined it was Tyrone's large hands manhandling me.

"Come on man! Let's get her drunk and see if she caves in! It worked in college!"

"Alright we can try tomorrow afternoon at the BBQ man, but don't get your hopes up or anything."

Before the messages ended, Tyrone sent my husband a picture of his black cock. I couldn't believe it! It must have been at least 12 inches. The veins bulged out around the shaft. I wanted to suck on his bulbous head so bad!

I put my husband's phone down and looked at the boys. They thought they were so devious! That must have been why Tyrone insisted I try his 'special' long island iced tea.

I couldn't believe my husband wanted me to fuck his big black friend. It was like the ultimate dream. I didn't want to let the boys get into me so easily though. After all a girl's gotta make them work for it, right? One thing was for certain; Tyrone was going to fuck me silly tonight!

After a few moments, I finally had enough of just lounging around. I need to set Tyrone's plan in motion. I got up and walked towards the boys. I lowered my bikini top so my nipples were barely covered. I'm sure that would get their attention pretty quick.

"Alright is the food ready yet? You boys talk more than a bunch of chicks at a book club."

The boys turned around and seemed fixated on my breasts. I gave them an intoxicating smile. This would be easier than taking candy from a baby.

"We're just about ready. What do you want?"

"Hmmm. I think I'll take a big old hotdog, Tyrone." I licked my lips as I brandished a seductive grin.

"U-uh sure thing. Why don't you go inside and I'll bring it in?"

"Good boy." I replied.

The look on the boys' faces was priceless! I knew after that exchange Tyrone's libido would be through the roof.

The boys brought back the food onto our dining room table. I made sure to eat the hotdog like I would a big cock. The boys could hardly contain themselves at the table.

"So Olivia, do you want another one of my patented long island ice teas?" Tyrone announced.

"Actually I think I'll go for a class of wine. You boys want anything?"

"I'll take a beer." My husband replied.

"Nah I'm good." Tyrone said. I knew he wanted to stay sober to fuck me.

"Okay I'll be right back from the kitchen.

As I left through the kitchen doors I pressed my ear against the door. The boys were star struck!

"Oh my god I think she wants me! Did you see how she ate that hotdog? I want her to do that to my cock tonight."

"Alright, calm you horses man. Don't scare her off and ruin this for the both of us!"

I laughed as the boys got all riled up. My pussy was dripping wet in anticipation of my first black cock.

"Okay okay. Shhhh I think she's coming back!"

I entered through the threshold of the living room with our new drinks. As dinner went on, Tyrone became more and more flirtatious. At first he grazed my hand, and then he put his manly hands on my thigh and caressed my pale white skin.

"You know Jim, your wife sure does get more beautiful every time I see her."

I blushed at Tyrone's obvious attempt at a compliment. His hand grazed my leg as goose bumps appeared on my arms.

"Yep she sure is a firecracker, aren't you honey?"

"Oh I'm much more than that." I said with a devilish grin. "You know what boys, it's getting pretty late. Short of a threesome I think I'm going to get some sleep."

A confused look appeared on the boy's faces. After all, I had just given them what we all wanted on a silver platter.

"Alright, no takers? Well I'm off then." I turned around and slipped off my panties, letting them drop to the floor before kicking them back. They landed in Tyrone's lap, who gasped like he had just seen a ghost.

My husband laughed. He came up and grabbed me, kissing me on the lips. "You read my emails didn't you?" His warm lips slid into me. His tongue pressed against my lips. It felt so good. He finally figured me out!

"I sure did. And you know what? I want your friend's big black cock. He's going to pleasure me in ways you never will."

I knew the dirty language Jim wanted to hear. I pushed my husband back. "Come on boys, if you want to fuck me you better hurry up." I playfully slapped my husband's ass as Tyrone carried me up the stairs in glee to our bedroom.

Chapter 2

Tyrone dropped me gently on the bed. Both boys looked down on me with big smiles on their faces.

"Take off your shorts, Tyrone. Let me see that big black cock."

Tyrone could hardly contain himself. He unbuckled his belt and dropped his shorts to the floor. He kicked them away in a hurry. His monster cock sprung to attention. It was 12 inches just like in the picture I saw earlier. Jim's eyes widened in surprise.

"Dang man you're going to put that thing in my wife?"

"Your damn right. I'm going to fuck her pussy into oblivion!"

I giggled at Tyrone's enthusiastic reaction. In response, I slowly slipped off my bikini top. My hard nipples bounced in the air as the boys almost fainted.

Jim moved in to grasp my breasts. I slapped his hand away.

"Don't be rude, Jim. Let our handsome guest enjoy me first."

Tyrone could hardly contain himself. He moved forward to caress my nipples in his large, gorilla-like hands while my husband removed his clothes. He was an average build, certainly nothing like Tyrone's incredible peak physical stature.

Our big black bull caressed my boobs in his hands. "How do you like them, Tyrone?"

"I love them." He moaned. His cock only got bigger.

"Yeah? Are you going to fuck me? Fuck my slutty pussy?"

"Yeah, I'm going to destroy it!"

I giggled at Tyrone's response. I wanted him so bad, but first I wanted to suck his monster cock. I got on my knees at the edge of the bed. "Let me suck your big black cock."

Tyrone held his cock in front of my lips; it was only inches away. I could almost taste his manhood.

"Pull my hair back sweetie." I directed at my husband. He

obeyed as commanded.

"Yeah, I want you to suck on my cock. Take it now!" Tyrone playfully slapped my cheek before he rammed his manhood down my throat. It was so big; I never experienced anything like it in my life.

I felt the think veins on the side of his cock slide against my tongue. My pussy dripped wet with pleasure. "Ohhh!" I moaned loudly.

My husband's fingers caressed my breasts for a moment, before moving down to my wet slit. His fingers worked magic on my little bean.

"Yeah suck that cock! Suck my black cock!"

I focused my attention on Tyrone's head. My tongue flicked it around as he grunted into the ceiling. His eyes closed as I pleasured him. I dragged my tongue from the tip of his cock to the base. Then I popped his balls in my mouth and threw them around. They were bigger than golf balls.

Meanwhile, Jim worked my pussy into a frenzy. Every

sensation became elevated as I continued to worship Tyrone's big black manhood. "Oh god! I love your cock! It's so big!"

"How much do you like it?!"

"I love it!"

Jim brought his lips down to my wet fold as I sucked off his ebony companion. He sucked on my little bud as I moaned into Tyrone's massive manhood. His tongue worked wonders on me. I could feel my inevitable orgasm building up.

"Lick my ass!" I bellowed at my husband. He quickly adjusted his position and attacked my tight little hole. His tongue darted in and out as his fingers fucked my pussy furiously.

"Ohhh! God! Oh my god!" I moaned.

"Olivia sure does know how to suck cock man! You're a lucky guy!" Tyrone commented.

Tyrone grabbed the back of my throat and rammed his large cucumber into my mouth rapidly. I gagged on his monster. I couldn't resist any longer. My pussy contracted as I experienced the most intense orgasm of my life. It was so strong I pushed my husband's fingers out of my pussy. His tongue continued to worship my ass.

My pussy juices rolled out like an over-flooded river.

"Oh god! She just came man!"

My husband quickly licked his fingers, tasting my sweet pussy juices. I pulled Tyrone's cock out of my mouth as I gasped for air. His cock tasted better than I could have ever imagined. He took my black cock virginity and I only wanted more.

"Lay down, I want to fuck your pussy." Tyrone announced.

Jim looked over at me with a big smile on his face. I knew his dirtiest fantasies were coming true. He wanted his wanton wife taken by his big black friend.

"Spread her legs for me." Tyrone commanded my husband.

Jim's fingers shook as he grabbed my knees and pushed my legs out. I was wide open to receive Tyrone's missile.

"You want this?!" Tyrone's voice boomed in our bedroom. His hand shook his 12 inch cock side to side.

I nodded in acknowledgment. "YES! I want your big black cock in me!"

"That's a gooood girl!" He purred.

Tyrone teased me by only pressing his bulbous black head against my little clit. I could literally feel the head of his cock pulse against me.

"Oh suck on my tits, honey." I grabbed my husband by the hair and forced his face down into my cleavage. My nipples were rock hard and I wanted them played with.

Jim didn't hesitate as he covered my right nipple with his mouth. He sucked down like it would be the last thing he would do. I arched my head back in pleasure. My eyes rolled to the back of my head. My left hand flicked my other nipple as Tyrone continued to tease me from below.

"Oh fuck me Tyrone! I need it!"

"Tell me why you need my cock." He said with a smug voice.

"I need black cock in me for the first time! Please! Take my big black cock virginity!"

"That's what I like to hear slut!" He slapped my ass playfully.

Tyrone pulled my body halfway off the edge of the bed and inserted his cock into my temple. I could feel his cock pulse in the walls of my pussy.

"Oh you're so big!" I screamed.

"Yeah you better be ready for this."

"Yes! Keep going!"

Tyrone hadn't even pushed his cock halfway in yet and he was already filling me up more than my husband ever did. It felt so hot having black cock in my pussy for the first time. My walls hugged his cock tight like a wrapper.

Every inch vibrated against my walls sending unimaginable shivers of pleasure to my brain. "Oh god!" I moaned. I came on Tyrone's big black cock just as the base of his shaft pushed against my clit.

My stomach tightened as my whole body trembled in pleasure. My dirty cunt wanted to squeeze the life out of Tyrone's massive cock. Jim watched with great excitement as I just came on his friend's cock.

"Ready to be fucked?"

"Yes! Please!" I begged Tyrone.

He grabbed onto my waist as his cock powered in and out of my pussy. His large balls slammed against my ass. My dirty cunt made loud, wet sucking sounds as he pounded me like a common whore.

"Oh god!"

My husband sucked on my other nipple. I grabbed his head and pushed it down. His cock was rock hard and I knew he loved every second of this.

Tyrone fucked me harder and faster. It seemed like he was trying to split my body in half. His cock put me in a mixing state of pleasure and pain. I had never had anything so big in me in my life.

The tip of his cock struck at my clit again and I shudder in another climax. My clit became more tender and sensitive. My legs thrashed around as I screamed like a banshee.

"Ohhhh! Ooooohhhh GOD!"

I could feel my pussy juices leak out into my asshole. I made a mental note to make Jim like it up later like a dog. I grabbed my husband's cock and jerked it. He had never been harder in his life. My hand squeezed the life out of his cock as Tyrone drilled me.

"Yeah! You're like a real whore!" Tyrone said to me.

"Yes! I'm your dirty whore!" I replied back. "Cum in my pussy! Cum in me now!"

"You want my black seed?!"

"YES!!!!"

Tyrone's cock seemed to grow in me as I begged him to cum.

"Oh!" He grunted. I knew wouldn't last much longer in my tight pussy. I flexed my stomach and pussy to really clamp down on his manhood.

"Here it comes! Oh god!" Tyrone announced.

By this point, I had jerked Jim into an orgasm. He came all over our pillows.

Meanwhile I could feel Tyrone's pulse in my pussy. His cock throbbed and he let everything loose.

"Yes! Oh! Oh yeah!" I moaned.

Tyrone's warm cum filled me up as I reached yet another orgasm. His black seed coated my entire unprotected pussy.

I grabbed my husband's hair and pulled him closer. "You're going to clean that cum from my pussy, faggot!"

A big smile appeared on Jim's face. I knew that's what he wanted.

Eventually Tyrone pulled out of my pussy. He lay in bed next to me as we stared at each other. His cum dripped out of my pussy onto the sheets.

"Clean me up." I snapped my fingers at Jim.

Jim practically jumped onto the bed to clean my dirty clit. He sucked around my inner thighs first before going for the gold mine.

His warm tongue drilled into my cum-filled pussy. "Oh that's a good boy!" I cried out.

Tyrone moved in close and kissed me on the lips. His big, warm lips swallowed me alive. His teeth grazed my bottom lips as I shuddered. Meanwhile, Jim's tongue moved into my ass to clean the cum that had dripped down.

"Can you taste him?" I wiggled my hips from side to side as my husband ate me out like a pro.

"Yes, I love it!" He muffled back. His lips were filled of the sweet nectar of our mixed juices. Jim continued to eat my pussy out until it was totally clean.

After he finished, Jim crawled up and we embraced for a passionate embrace. I could taste Tyrone's yummy black cock on my husband's lips. I loved it.

Jim checked the time. "Well, I guess we should probably go to bed, right?"

The boys glanced at me as a devious smiled formed across my face. "We could do that...or you boys can fuck me senseless. It's up to you...

I bent over with my ass and pussy up high. I knew the boys wouldn't be able to resist! I was going to be a good whore for Tyrone while my husband watched!

Straying Wife: Hotwife Secret

Jenni Winters

Chapter 1

She was gone again. Where did she go at this hour?

I watched from our window as my wife, Lexi, left the house. For the past week she would leave at some ungodly hour to god knows where. She didn't usually get back until early in the morning before I woke up.

This time I wanted to figure out where she was going. I rushed downstairs for my car to tail behind her.

I was careful to stay far enough away so she wouldn't notice me. My heart beat faster and faster. I think deep down I knew what was going on. I didn't want to admit it, but maybe she was actually cheating on me.

We didn't have to travel far. She pulled into a nice, upscale cul-de-sac.

My wife wore a sexy pair of yoga pants and a tank top. It was still pretty warm under the night summer sky. Luckily it was pitch black outside. I parked across the street as she walked up to the unknown house.

A large man answered the door. I couldn't make out his face from this far away.

What the fuck was going on? When he opened the door, she reached up and kissed him. My heart nearly fell out of my chest.

How could Lexi cheat on me like this? When they went into his place thoughts filled my head. My mind was spinning so fast I thought I would vomit.

I had to get a better look. I had to find out more. Why was this happening to me?

I slowly ran up to the mystery man's porch. "Is Jeremy asleep?"

"Yep. He's sleeping like a baby. Don't worry, Bruce, you have me all to yourself."

He hugged my wife as they embraced for another kiss. I watched in the bushes like some kind of peeping tom. I wanted to barge in and kick that guy's ass, but he looked to be at least a foot taller than me.

In fact, he could pass for a NBA player. He was ripped and handsome, the ultimate deadly combination.

"Mmmm I'm so glad you called me." He whispered as my wife nibbled on his neck. They were getting hot and steamy on his couch.

"I'm glad too. Jeremy just can't satisfy me. His dick is just too small."

What? Lexi never mentioned that to me. I was reevaluating my entire existence. It was the most painful night of my life, yet I still couldn't turn away. I watched closely as he made love to my wife.

Bruce slowly unwrapped my wife like a Christmas present. He sucked on her nipples as she groaned.

"Oh Bruce! I need your big cock in me!"

"Yeah? Let me hear you beg for it."

"Please fuck me, Bruce. I need your cock!"

My heart skipped a beat as my wife begged for another man's cock. I wanted to run away, but something compelled me to stay. Just as inexplicably, my cock hardened as my wife knelt down on the floor and pulled his sweat pants down.

I pulled down my own pants as well and began to jerk off a little. It was just my natural reaction. I couldn't explain it and I couldn't fight it.

She pulled out his massive big black cock. He must have been three times my size. "Oh yes! That's what I'm talking about!"

My wife was obviously excited. She held his cock in her hand and stroked. "Suck on it." He ordered.

Lexi bobbed up and down on his cock. She chocked on it as he held her head down. "Yeah! That's it!" Bruce groaned.

"Fuck me! Please fuck me!"

"Yeah, I'm going to destroy that tiny pussy of yours!"

Bruce pulled my wife onto his lap and lowered her slowly onto his manhood. My wife screamed like a ghost. I had never seen her like that before. It made me feel so pathetic and miserable.

I couldn't take much more of this. I left the bushes and rushed home. I just couldn't watch them have sex like that.

~~~

Lexi came back a few hours later. "Hey babe, are you still awake?"

I felt her cold body climb into the sheets. She pressed her lips on my cheek.

"Yeah..." I said coldly. I hadn't been able to sleep all night ever since I found out she was cheating on me.

"Something wrong?" She asked innocently.

"I followed you out tonight." I told her bluntly.

"You what?"
~~~

"I saw you and Bruce having sex." I continued.

"Well it's about time you found out." She said with a giggle.

"What's so funny?"

"I saw you tailing me in your car. You thought you were being discreet but you weren't." She replied.

"What? Really?"

"Yeah I know. I saw you jerking off in the bushes too." She said. Lexi changed her voice to be more seductive.

She straddled me on the bed and dug her nails into my chest. "You liked it didn't you? You liked seeing another man take me."

"What? You're crazy!" I spat out.

"Really?"

Lexi lifted the sheets and reached back. She grabbed my hardon. "I think you like this. You like seeing me cheat on you. You know your tiny dick would never fully please me, right?"

I didn't even know what to say at this point. I was absolutely speechless.

"Come on! Don't deny it, baby! Tell me you love it!"

She began to kiss my neck. I moaned in response.

"Oh god..."

"Say it! Tell me how much you like it!"

"Oh god! I love it..."

I couldn't believe I actually said that. That I actually admitted that.

"You love seeing me with another man, right?"

"Yes!" I finally admitted. I felt like a boulder had been lifted off my chest.

"That's good cause I want to fuck Bruce again already. He's so much bigger than you. You didn't stay for the entire thing, right?"

"No..." I replied.

"Good. Cause tomorrow night I'm going over to his place again. And you're going to watch him take me."

"Oh my god..." I replied.

"Better get some rest. You're going to have one wild night!" Lexi playfully slapped my face. I didn't get much sleep that night. I didn't know if it was because of the stress or excitement.

Chapter 2

"Are you nervous, honey?"

Lexi reached over and caressed my cheek.

"A little..."

"Don't worry, Bruce is a nice guy. He's actually my trainer at the gym. You'll enjoy this, don't worry."

Lexi caressed my crotch as I moaned. She softly tapped on it and smiled. "Let's go. I'm ready for his big black dick now."

I felt like we walked a mile from the sidewalk to Bruce's porch. My heart felt heavy every step of the way. It would be so humiliating to ask him to let me watch as they had sex. I mean it was all pretty crazy.

We knocked on the door. Bruce answered. He absolutely towered over me. I felt inferior right away.

"Hi, baby!" Lexi went up and hugged her lover. They embraced for a kiss.

"Bruce, I'd like to you to meet my husband, Jeremy. Jeremy, this is Bruce."

We shook hands. He crushed my fingers with his large gorilla hands. I tried to hide my obvious physical pain.

"Hi..."

"Hello..."

There was an awkward silence until Lexi broke it up. "He found out baby. But don't worry. All he wants to do is watch. Isn't that right, Jeremy?"

"Uh...yes..." I replied. I must have turned bright red instantly.

Bruce didn't even bat an eye. He looked at me and chuckled. "Well, I guess that's fine. I don't really even care. Come in. I've been so horny for you, Lexi."

We entered his place. It was a nice modest home. My wife wore a similar outfit to yesterday: yoga pants and a tank.

"Hmmm!"

Bruce was aggressive right off the bat. He assaulted my wife with kisses. He dragged her to the couch again and lay on top of her.

"Oh yes! I love how warm your lips are!"

My cock hardened in my jeans. I rubbed it from the outside. I couldn't believe I was actually enjoying this.

Bruce dug into her tank and pulled out her breasts. He sucked on her tits. My wife arched her head back and moaned. "Oh Bruce!"

They were getting hot and heavy fast. He pulled off her shirt and went for her pants next. My wife wore a sexy pink thong underneath.

Bruce slipped it off slowly with his mouth. "Smell how wet she is for me!"

He tossed her panties to me. I grabbed them off the floor

and inhaled the crotch. They were damp to the touch. Her sweet nectar filled my nose. I couldn't get enough.

I smelled them like my life depended on it. I was in heaven. I dropped my jeans to the floor and pulled out my hard cock.

Luckily Bruce hadn't noticed how small I was compared to him yet.

He focused his attention on my wife now. His face bore down as he ate her out. "Oh god!" My wife moaned.

Lexi's hips gyrated from side to side as he pleasured her. His tongue flicked her clit as she screamed. She grabbed his hair and pushed his head back down.

"God! That feels so good, honey!"

Lexi and I locked eyes. I jerked off my cock as she smiled seductively at me. "Enjoying this?" She whispered at me.

All I could do was nod my head. She smiled and focused her attention on Bruce again. "Fuck me, baby! Fuck me now!"

Bruce unbuckled his pants as Lexi pulled them down. His big cock jumped out of his boxers. I saw it from a distance last night, but it was insane being so close to it now. Bruce must have been 10 inches long.

"Jesus Christ!" I muttered under my breath.

"Now that's a real cock!" My wife commented. "Come here and take a look."

I walked over and knelt by the couch. My face was a mere inches away from his massive big black cock. I still couldn't believe he was so much bigger than me.

"Keep jerking your cock, honey. I want you to get off as he's fucking me."

"Yes, honey." I replied.

Bruce sprung into action rapidly. He mounted my wife and pushed his cock into her.

Lexi's nails dug into the couch. I couldn't even believe

she could take something so big. "Oh god!" She screamed.

Bruce inched himself deeper and deeper as my wife groaned.

"Fuck me harder, Bruce! Fuck me harder!"

Bruce smiled and held onto my wife's waist. He rammed his cock up her cunt. The entire couch moved back and forth as they fucked.

"Oh yes!" My wife groaned. It was like she had transformed into another person.

He was absolutely an animal. I had never seen anyone fuck so hard before. My wife's pussy began to swell up. She was taking a beating from this animal.

"Fuck! Yes!"

"Oh my god..." I whispered. I had no idea it would be like this. For some reason my cock only turned harder.

"God! That feels so good!" My wife screamed.

My cock only throbbed as she moaned for another man. "Cum in me! Please cum in me, Bruce!"

"Yeah? You want my hot cum?!"

"Yes! Please!"

"Beg harder!"

"Please cum in her, sir!" I blurted out. I got so caught up in the moment that I couldn't even control myself anymore. I just wanted to see him do it...to see him deflower my very own wife.

Bruce chuckled. "Ha ha. You got it, sucker! I'm going to cum so hard in your wife!"

Bruce thrust his manhood faster and faster into my wife. Lexi grunted with every thrust. "Oh yes! Oh yes!"

It was so amazing to watch it all unfold. "Yes! I'm going to cum in you!"

"Do it! Do it!" Lexi screamed.

Bruce fucked my wife one last time before he busted his load. I couldn't hold back any longer. I came into my wife's panties as another man came in my wife's cunt.

"Oh! Oh!" I groaned.

I nearly blacked out. It was the most intense orgasm of my life. I couldn't believe how hot this all was.

"Clean me out, Jeremy." My wife pulled my head down. Her pussy was a mess. It was completely covered with Bruce's man jizz.

I slurped it up like my life depended on it. His cum was still warm. It tasted like salty water. My tongue massaged all over her folds.

"Yes! That's the spot." Lexi groaned. She seemed so happy.

"I love you."

"I love you too." I replied. It was the truth. Lexi had just cheated on me, but we had never been closer. I loved her to death. I didn't care if another man pleasured her. All I wanted was to be with her.

After we cleaned up, I whisked her back to the car and drove home. The quiet drive home was the highlight of our trip. We held hands in silence and embraced the moment. It was the start to a new chapter in our marriage.

The Hotwife Experience

Jenni Winters

Chapter 1

The ride to downtown was smooth. I sat in the warm leather seat of our limo. My palms gripped my husband's as they began to sweat. My heart raced so fast I thought I would pass out. Our marriage was about to go to a place we had never gone before.

For years my husband, Josh, begged me to fulfill his greatest fantasy. I was highly reluctant for the longest time. I mean cheat on my husband? My parents didn't raise me like that. It sounds crazy, right?

I've always been a prim and proper housewife like my mother and her mother before her. I mean it was just how the world worked. However, Josh had the inexplicable fantasy he needed to realize. He wanted me to be taken by a big black man.

I couldn't believe him when he first told me about his fetish. I thought it was some kind of joke. I mean he wanted his tiny, white wife to take a black cock?

After Josh told me about his fantasy we had some of the hottest sex in our marriage. We watched the dirtiest interracial porn together. It made me so wet thinking about getting drilled by a 12 inch monster.

Josh even ordered a big black dildo online that we played with. These days, the dildo fucked me more than he did. I guess eventually things needed to get more real. The porn and the role playing with the dildo became old and stale.

I really wanted a black cock for myself. I had girlfriends in college that told me it was the best thing since sliced bread. They told me how black men are so much better lovers than white guys. They said once you go black you never go back.

Josh's hand caressed my knee. The driver looked back through the mirror and smiled. I blushed in embarrassment. I wore an elegant red dress that showed off my melons. I even had matching red lipstick for the special occasion. He must have thought I was a high end hooker or something. I guess it was true in some regard.

"Are you okay, Jessie?"

"I'll be okay. I'm just...you know a little nervous."

"Don't be. I'll be there all the way with you."

"I know. I bet you're hard right now too."

I moved my hand over and caressed Josh's crotch. I felt his rock hard dick. He was really enjoying this. My husband smiled back at me. His greatest dream was about to be realized.

I couldn't believe this was about to happen. This meeting had been on my mind the entire week. You see, our neighbor and good friend, Marie, put us in contact with a black bull, Eli.

He was a successful tech entrepreneur who had a big fantasy. He loved to fuck housewives who had never had black cock before. He loved to take their black virginity. It was exactly what we were looking for. I wanted him to forcibly take me and make me his. It made my pussy wet.

Josh and I were headed for his downtown penthouse. It would overlook the city so we would have a pretty good view while he drilled me. We didn't really know what to expect. I mean we had never done something like this before.

We finally reached our destination. "Alright, here you are." Our driver announced. "As a word of advice, don't sweat it too much. Just have fun." He said.

I couldn't believe this. How many girls had this man deflowered before?

"Are you sure you want to go through with this?" My husband asked me one last time.

"I'm sure. I want him."

Josh and I held hands as we entered the building. The doorman opened the door for us. The lobby of this mixed development building was beautiful. Shiny black marble coated the floor. Chandeliers hung from the glass sky. It was a marvel.

We went straight for the elevator. "What floor?" The man asked us.

"Suite 65." My husband answered.

The man hit a button off on the side and the elevator ascended to the heavens. My stomach felt like it was tied in knots. Soon enough, we reached Eli's suite. It certainly looked extravagant and fit for a king. We rang the door as the elevator went back down.

"Maybe he's not home." I said quietly.

We waited for another fifteen seconds before the handle turned. A tall, dark, and handsome man answered the door.

"Hi, you must be Josh and Jessie." He said in a deep voice. "I'm Eli."

He took my hand in his dark paws. His flesh was warm. I blushed when he looked me in the eyes. I was completely speechless.

"H-Hi. I-I'm Jessie."

"Pleasure to meet you." He said and kissed my ring. It made me so wet with pleasure.

He was certainly very attractive. He wore a black dress shirt and slacks. However, I could see his very ripped body underneath. It couldn't wait to rip off his clothes and really admire his muscles.

Josh and Eli shook hands as he invited us in. "Your wife looks absolutely ravishing." He said.

Josh could barely contain his excitement. The inside of Eli's penthouse was absolutely amazing. He had a 360 degree view of the city. People looked like ants from up here. We were literally in the clouds.

Everything looked so ornate in his home. He had several love seats spread around the place and a large king sized bed in a corner. I wondered if that's where he intended to ravage my body.

"Would you two like a drink." He said.

"Uh sure." I replied. A little liquid courage sure would calm my stomach before.

Eli poured us an expensive brand of cognac. I tasted the heavenly nectar. It warmed my entire body as it made its way down my stomach. Eli looked at us the way a lion stalked its prey.

"So are you ready to be fucked by me, Jessie." Eli said at

me.

Chapter 2

My husband laughed at Eli's frankness.

"Yes! She's ready for you. It's the only thing she's talked about all week!"

"That's good. When your neighbor told me about you I knew I had to have you." He said in a smooth voice. His fingers grazed my cheek.

I became mesmerized with is dark eyes and handsome face. "I want you." I whispered.

I leaned in close and smelled his cologne. It smelled like fine Italian leather. I couldn't get enough of it. I leaned in closer and we locked lips. They were so soft. We made large sucking noises as he put down his drink on the counter.

Josh was probably in heaven right now. This large bull, towering at over six feet tall, had already begun his move. His tongue touched mine as we battled for dominance.

We broke our embrace for a moment. "That's a good girl. I

can tell you want this. Most girls that come here have to see my cock first before they succumb to their desires."

"Fuck me." I begged him. Fingers caressed his shoulders and found my way down to his firm ass. He was the most built man I had ever seen in my life.

"Is that what you want?" Eli asked my husband.

"More than anything." He replied with eagerness. "I want you to ruin my wife. I want you to destroy her pussy."

Those were the exact words Eli wanted to hear. "I'll do more than that. You'll never enjoy your wife's pussy again after this. Once she has my cock she'll never want yours again."

Eli lifted me up and walked towards his bed. "Let's get you out of this dress into something more comfortable." He said with a chuckle. Josh followed us like a puppy dog.

He placed me on the bed as I kissed him again. He landed on top of me. His broad chest pushed against my hard nipples. "Undress you little cuck." Eli ordered my husband.

Josh completely stripped down as ordered. Meanwhile, we continued to make out in front of him. Eli practically peed in his pants laughing when he saw my husband's pathetic dick. "Is that really how big he is?" He pointed at Josh.

"Unfortunately, yes." I replied. He was rock hard and only sported a five inch cock. It was nothing compared to the heat Eli packed. I could feel his cock press against me. "You're nothing compared to him baby." I mocked him.

My husband smiled as our hotwife adventure began. I could already see a little bit of pre-cum drip from his cock.

"Let's get this skimpy dress off." He said.

His hand reached over and unzipped my dress. He practically ripped it off and threw it to the distance. I pulled off his shirt and his buttons flew all over the place. "I love your chest." I whispered to him. My fingers ran over his dark flesh and caressed every single muscle. It was the hottest thing in the world.

My pussy was dripping wet at this point and he hadn't even fucked me. Eli ripped off my bra and my nipples flew all over the place. "You sure do have a hot wife, you cuck." He said to my husband.

"She is the best." He replied.

Eli sucked on my nipple immediately as his hand went for my panties. He moved it to the side and inserted his fingers into my holy temple. "Oh god!" I moaned.

Eli expertly fucked my pussy with his fingers while sucking on my nipples. I had never felt anything like this before. He was a man who really knew the female body. His fingers worked my clit as I orgasmed. My pussy almost pushed his fingers out, but he pushed back.

"Yes! Oh god! YES! FUCK me!" I begged him. "I need your cock!"

My husband couldn't believe Eli brought me to orgasm so fast. It usually took him at least half an hour. My pussy tingled with pleasure. I wanted more and more.

"Let me see your cock. Please, Eli."

Eli wiped my juices clean with my panties and threw them to my husband. "Here, enjoy this cuck, while I enjoy your wife."

Josh caught my panties and sniffed them like he was deprived of oxygen. Our black bull then stood up and dropped his pants. I could see his marvelous snake and it made me so wet. It was over 12 inches long. His dark steel rod would be destroying my dainty pussy. No amount of practice with that black dildo could have prepared me for the real thing.

"Oh it's so big." Josh whispered.

"I know. It's so beautiful."

"Are you ready to get fucked by black cock for the first time?" He asked me.

"Yes! I want it...but I think our cuck needs to wet it first." I said with a devious smile and looked back at my husband.

"Well, what are you waiting for?" Eli ordered. He placed his hands on his hips as Josh kneeled down before a superior black man.

"Suck his cock for me, baby! Suck the thing that will be giving me so much pleasure." I whispered in his ear.

"Anything you say." He said with a smile. I grabbed my husband's head and shoved it into Eli's cock. Josh had never sucked cock before, but I knew he was enjoying this. I could already hear him gag a few inches in. He sure wasn't an experienced cock sucker like me.

"How does it taste, cuck!"

"Mmmm!" He said while still stuffed with big black cock.

"How is he sucking on your cock?"

"He's no good." Eli replied.

I had to change that! I knelt down with Josh and we shared Eli's cock together. "This is how you suck cock baby." I rolled my tongue around Eli's big head. I tasted Eli's wonderful manhood. I felt his body shudder in pleasure as I worked magic on him.

"Yes! Your cuck needs to learn to be a better fluffer!"

"Work on his balls honey, while I take care of the rest." Josh diligently sucked on Eli's big golf sized balls, while I really deep throated his cock.

"Oh!" He moaned from above. I felt his muscles tighten above. Josh and I held hands as we pleasured him. It was the most erotic and romantic experience in our marriage. Eli's cock tasted so good. I just wanted to have more and more!

He grabbed the back of my head and thrust forward. "You're a good little slut aren't you!"

"Yes! I'm your slut! Fuck me! Fuck my tiny white pussy!"

Eli laughed. He was ready for the main event. Josh and I both stopped sucking on his genitals. Eli picked me up and threw me on the bed again. He jumped on top of me and we embraced for a kiss. Meanwhile, our cuck sucked on my toes. My husband knew exactly what I liked. Things were going to another level from here.

Chapter 3

"Mmm!" I moaned while Eli and I kissed. His massive hands pleasured my seed from below. My husband sucked my toes from the edge of the bed. I felt his tongue caress every individual toe. He was a much better toe sucker than a cock sucker.

"Fuck me!" I whispered to our black bull. "I want your big black cock in me!"

"You want it BAD don't you?!"

"Yes! I want it so much!"

"I'm going to ruin your pussy! You hear that cuck?! You'll never enjoy your wife again!"

"Please fuck her!" Josh said excitedly.

Eli positioned the tip of his cock on my clit and pushed it in. "Oh!" My eyes rolled all the way back as his magnificent spear penetrated below.

"God!" I screamed. I looked down and only the tip of his

head was in me. It was going to be really rough. "Keep going! Please!" I begged him.

Eli continued to push his massive cock deeper and deeper into my pussy. "Yes! Oh yes!"

"You sure do have a tight cunt!" Eli whispered to me. He was about halfway in. The pain was so unbearable I screamed. However, I also felt a great deal of pleasure. Eli kissed me to muffle my screams. Josh watched in horror as our black bull defiled the sanctity of our marriage.

"Mmmggh!" I moaned into his mouth. Eli pushed and pushed. My hips gyrated from side to side as he penetrated me. A flood of juices gushed out of my pussy. My pussy contracted on his large cock. I had my second amazing orgasm of the day. "Oh!" I moaned softly. We continued to lock lips.

All of a sudden I felt the base of Eli's cock rest against my clit. "You're all the way in." I whispered.

"Are you ready?" He asks me.

"Yes! Fuck me! Fuck me with your black cock!"

Eli smiled as he placed his hands on the bed. His hips rocked forward sending shivers across my body.

"Oh! Yes! I've never felt like this before!" I could feel every single movement of his big black cock. My pussy stretched out far to accommodate his monstrous rod.

"You love this don't you!"

"It's the best!"

I looked down and Josh was in complete awe as Eli's member rocked my world. It was a mix of pain and pleasure. My husband's cock would never make me feel like this. Eli turned me around. "I want to fuck you like a dog!" He whispered in a dominant voice.

"Yes! Fuck me!"

Eli shoved his giant cock forcibly into me this time. I groaned as he re-entered my body. He grabbed my hips and thrust forward like a jackhammer. With every lunge forward his cock flicked my clit. I couldn't hold back any longer and my pussy contracted as I experienced yet another orgasm. I felt my insides squeeze against his warm cock.

I rubbed my fingers against my clit. It was wet with our mixed juices. I took a sniff and it drove me crazy. I knew my husband was probably dying for a taste.

I looked over at Josh who seemed to be in a deep trance. "Come here cuck! Lick my clit while he fucks me!"

Josh scurried over her like a dog. He lay perpendicular to me as his tongue caressed my clit. "Yes! That's a good cuck! Suck on that!"

His warm lips sucked down on my bead. I squirmed as Eli fucked me from behind. His large hands completely manhandled me. Goosebumps filled my arms. My husband's cock stood at attention. His little pecker amused me. It was no match for Eli's real manhood.

"Cum in me! Cum in my dirty cunt!" I shouted behind to our black bull.

"You're one dirty slut!" He shouted back at me.

He grabbed my hips and went into over-drive. His big black cock rammed in and out faster than ever. My pussy was already swollen beyond belief and would likely remain so for several days if not weeks. I could barely contain my excitement for the inevitable explosion.

"Are you ready!"

"Yes! Cum in me!"

A few more thrusts came and Eli finally exploded. I felt him spray his superior seed inside me. My husband timed it perfectly and sucked hard on my clit. I placed my hand on his head, pushing him deeper. "Oh god!" I screamed. I came again as Eli continued to fuck me even though he had just cum.

"Oh god! Oh god! Oh god!" I repeated. It was the most intense sexual experience I had ever been a part of.

"Lick her clean!" Eli ordered my husband.

"Yes sir." He said. Eli pulled out and his cum dripped out of my pussy like a waterfall. Josh went in quick and sucked everything up.

"Let me see you swallow it!" I told him.

Josh lifted his head up and swallowed Eli's cum like a good little cuck. "That's a good boy." I cooed at him. Eli cuddled up against me and we shared a warm embrace. His lips found mine and we kissed passionately while Josh cleaned me up.

"How was your first black cock experience?" Eli asked me.

"Oh it was so amazing! I'll never go back to white cock now!"

"Ha ha! That's what they all say. When your cuck is done cleaning you up, meet me in the shower. I want to cum all over your face." He ordered me.

Eli headed for the bathroom as Josh dutifully cleaned me up. "Did you enjoy this, honey?"

"Yes." He said, nodding his head.

"Good, because you're never fucking me again. From now on,

you only get the hotwife experience! I only want black cock from now on!"

Along For The Ride

Jenni Winters

Chapter 1

"How's your steak, Chris?"

"Oh...it's very good babe," I replied.

Victoria knew full well I was too preoccupied to be focused on the slab of meat in front of me. The hustle and bustle of the hotel restaurant seemed to be a distant noise.

All I could focus on was my wife and Mason. My wife had many lovers and Mason just so happened to be into town for the New Year.

"Mmm! That's the spot!"

Victoria closed her eyes and moaned softly as Mason parted her hair back and kissed her neck. He looked like a vampire feasting on its prey. My dick hardened against my pants. I loved watching my wife with other men. We had turned our little secret into a full blown lifestyle.

We've had some crazy nights traveling all over the world. I'm sure tonight would be no different.

"Hurry up and finish your steak, Chris. I'm going to go dancing with Mason soon," Victoria whispered into my ear. Mason stood up and excused himself to the bathroom.

I'm pretty sure the hairs on my arm stood straight up at attention. "Oh yeah?"

"Yes. I can't wait to rub against his crotch."

Underneath the table Victoria reached her fingers over and grabbed my crotch. She held my dick firmly in her hand.

"How does that feel?"

Her fingers danced around the fabric of my pants. I had to control myself after I thrust ever so slightly into her soft hands.

"It feels so good."

"I know..."

Her lips sucked on my earlobe. I sighed loudly. "I want his

cock so bad right now..."

Victoria's tongue explored around my ear. It felt so erotic. I didn't care that people were staring over here or what was going on in their minds. I was having the time of my life with the love of my life.

"Well, look whose back!"

"Care to dance, my love?" Mason extended his hand out and my wife accepted it. I smiled deviously at them.

"Get her back in one piece," I joked with Mason.

"No promises. She can be quite the firecracker," he replied back!

I went back to focus on my steak. I had only a quarter of it left. It was cooked to perfection. I began cutting into the meat while Mason led my wife to the dance floor. It was an incredible thing to watch from affair. The two of them sure did turn heads all over the restaurant and bar.

They danced the night away while I watched and ate. My wife

ground her ass into Mason's crotch. He must have been so hard. My wife was known to be quite the tease.

Victoria and Mason began making out. They were hot and heavy. He put his hand on her cheek and they exchanged tongues. His other hand grabbed her ass firmly as they danced to the beats of the music.

My wife looked incredible. She wore a strapless red dress. Her hair was curled and they bounced with every movement. Mason on the other hand looked rather dapper. He wore a simple suit and blue tie. He could certainly light up a room just like my wife.

He spun my wife around. They danced with such vigor and passion. I knew things would be going upstairs very soon. I poured the last drops of wine into my glass and enjoyed the show.

I had already had a few drinks so I was feeling pretty buzzed at this point.

When I had finished the last piece of steak the two of them had finished dancing. Victoria came up and pulled on my collar.

I could smell Mason's cologne on her skin. It smelled ravishing on my own wife.

"Hey babe, can you take care of the bill? We're going to go upstairs first."

"Sure thing."

Victoria leaned in and kissed me. I didn't mind that her lips were on Mason moments before. She patted my crotch before leaving in Mason's arms.

I went straight for the waiter right away. I didn't want to miss any of the action. "Hey can we please get the check please?"

"Sure thing sir."

The guy seemed to take forever. I had grown inpatient so I took out my wallet and pulled out all the cash I could. Then, I went straight for the elevator.

The ride up took a long time. We had gotten a nice suite for the entire weekend. I figured it would come in handy as we spent most of the day exploring around the downtown area.

I ran towards our room. They had left the door creaked open slightly for me.

"Oh yes!"

I could hear my own wife moaning from the other side. My cock twitched uncontrollably. I just loved it when she moaned another man's name.

I walked across the threshold. The two of them were already in bed together. Their legs were intertwined between the sheets. Their clothes were scattered all over the floor.

"Come suck on my toes Chris," my wife beckoned me.

I knelt at the edge of the bed and popped her big toe into my mouth. Meanwhile, I could hear sucking noises from the top of the bed. I figured they were kissing.

Her toes tasted good. The bed rocked as my wife climbed on top of Mason. She threw the blankets off to the side. It was incredible to watch her on top of him. My cock throbbed as I knew what was about to happen.

Chapter 2

"Oh yes! I've missed your cock, Mason!"

Victoria grabbed onto his cock and rubbed it against her cunt. She rubbed it back and forth the length of his manhood. "Fuck! You're so wet!"

"I know..."

"Come watch Chris..."

I lay on the bed right next to Mason and stripped down naked. I watched with such glee as my wife glided on his dick. She pushed it against his stomach with her cunt and rode it. He groaned softly.

I held her hand as she thrust forward and back on his cock. "Put it in..." I whispered.

"Patience," she replied with a smile.

Mason was in absolute heaven. "Hold his dick up for me," she commanded me.

I couldn't resist that opportunity. I held Mason's dick up by the base. His skin was flaming hot. Victoria slowly lowered herself onto his cock until her lips grazed the tips of my fingers. "Oh yes! That's it!"

"Fuck me," Mason whispered to my wife.

A devilish grin appeared on Victoria's face. It was like she was possessed by another being. She rode him like a mad woman.

She placed her hands on his shoulders and rocked back and forth. I could hear their hips collide into one another. I could tell Victoria was soaking wet.

She pushed down on him. Her nails dug into his skin. It was incredible to watch.

"I love your cock!"

She was breathing heavily. Her boobs bounced up and down as she fucked another man in front of me. I grabbed onto her breasts and rubbed them. They were so firm yet plush. I sucked on them as she groaned. I could feel her breath against my neck.

"Oh yes! Suck on it!"

My tongue twirled around her nipple. Victoria always did have sensitive nipples. She groaned and came on Mason's cock. Her whole body tensed up. She screamed in pleasure.

"God..." I remarked.

The bed was getting soaked. I didn't care though. The only thing on my mind was the pleasure Victoria received.

"Fuck me from behind!"

Mason smiled. He got up and behind my wife. He slapped his cock against her ass a few times. "Oh! Oh!"

Mason shoved his manhood in as my wife groaned. I held her face and we stared into each other's souls. "I love you."

"I love you too," she replied with a grin.

We smiled for a brief moment before Mason plunged his cock

deep into her cunt. His balls slapped back and forth as he fucked her.

I held Victoria in close. We kissed as he railed her from behind. I bit down softly on her lip as she sighed against me. We held hands as and enjoyed this incredibly erotic moment for all that it was worth.

"Oh yes! Oh yes! Come in me, baby!"

"Yeah? You want my cum?!"

Mason fucked my wife harder and harder. He even slapped her ass a few times. Victoria reached her fingers back and rubbed her clit vigorously. "Yes! I want your cum!"

"Fuck! Here is comes!"

Mason thrust faster and harder into my wife. She arched her head back. Mason finally let it all go and screamed. "Yes! I'm coming in you!"

He sounded like a wild animal. I don't know how many times he exploded into my wife, but my cock throbbed in response.

When he pulled out of Victoria I saw it all drip onto the bed. It was incredible. "Whew! I'm going to the bar to get some wine. You guys want anything?"

"Nope. Wine sounds good," I replied.

As Mason left, Victoria jumped on top of me. "Fuck me. I know you want to. Do it while his cum is still warm."

I grinned. Victoria knew exactly what I wanted. I pushed my cock into her. It felt so warm and damp in there. I loved the feeling of Mason's cum all around my cock.

"Fuck me, Chris!"

Her erotic voice beckoned me. I pushed my cock into her and we fucked. Victoria and I kissed. It was incredible. I wanted more and more. I fucked her as hard as I could. I knew I wouldn't last long at this pace.

Victoria bit down softly on my lip. "Cum in me, Chris. Do it! Do it!"

Victoria's sultry voice threw me over the edge. It was the most powerful orgasm I had ever had. My cock throbbed inside her warm cunt. I exploded like a volcano. I must have shot six or seven loads into her. We kissed as I exploded.

Her muffled lips moaned into my mouth. I savored the moment and inhaled the scent of her intoxicating perfume.

"Oh god!"

I dumped myself right next to her on the bed. We were both completely and utterly exhausted from the night. It was so incredible. What a way to start off the year!

Victoria and I cuddled. Our legs were intertwined and I felt the warmth of her skin against mine. "That feels so good," she whispered to me.

"I know. Thank you for a wonderful night."

"It's not over yet!" Mason walked back into the room with a bottle of wine and champagne. "The night is still young."

He poured us three glasses of champagne and we toasted each

other. "To an unforgettable night."

"To an unforgettable night," we exclaimed.

After a few sips, Mason was horny and ready to get back into action. I lay back with my eyes barely open. The last thing I remember was Victoria moaning his name loudly. It was intense and erotic. I wouldn't have it any other way.

Cuckolded By A Superior Couple

Jenni Winters

Chapter 1

"Oh my god! Stop it!" Allison giggled. I watched with jealously as Thompson playfully splashed water on my wife. The two of them were acting like little school kids. I wanted punch him so bad, but knew it would be a bad idea.

Thompson was huge. He was at least half a foot taller than me. Not to mention the fact that he looked like a ripped football player. I wasn't exactly fat, but I was no match for a man like him. His biceps looked bigger than my legs for god's sake.

Allison and I had decided to go on vacation to this adult resort in Hawaii. She had hounded me for years to come here. I finally gave in to her nagging. I wasn't exactly fond of the place because it attracted a certain darker crowd if you get my drift.

We were relaxing by the pool in the courtyard. It was a nice little area. There was a giant Olympic-sized pool in the middle and several nice cabanas off to the side. We had one of the best areas to the right.

From the first moment we walked in, I had only seen one or two other white people here. In fact, this place seemed to be only filled with big black men. I knew they would love my dainty little wife. She attracted so much attention from these guys.

I had the sneaking suspicion that my wife had a thing for black guys. She never said anything, but I always noticed how she would check them out in public. Plus, I had accidentally seen her porn history a few times. They were always of gang bangs with black guys.

Thompson walked up and carried my wife out of the pool like he was rescuing her from a boat crash. "Well thank you. You're such a gentleman." My wife giggled.

"So, Thompson, do you have a wife or girlfriend?" I asked crudely.

"Unfortunately not, Bart. I'm living the single dream." He replied.

"You're joking." My wife seemed surprised. "You're handsome, smart, and charming. I can't believe you haven't been snapped up yet." She slapped his stomach playfully. I figured she just wanted to touch his six pack in front of me. Thompson was truly a specimen of peak human performance.

"What can I say...I just haven't found the right person yet." He smiled at my wife and looked her in eyes.

"By the way Allison, let me put some sun screen on you. You shouldn't risk getting a sunburn." He seemed concerned over my wife.

"Well, sure if you insist."

Thompson gleefully squirted a hand-full of lotion onto his hand. "You know what, let me do it. I am here husband after all." I replied. I sure as hell wasn't going to let another man touch my wife as she wore basically nothing!

"It's okay Bart. I got this." Thompson said.

"I insist." I replied.

"Just let him do it, honey." Allison said in an annoyed voice.

I backed off right away, but felt pretty pissed off about it. Thompson rubbed his hands together and began to rub his dirty paws all over my wife as she lay on her stomach. He started with her legs and moved up to her ass. Allison moaned softly as his hands caressed her skin.

"So, Allison, have you ever been with a black man before?"

I was stunned by the frankness of Thompson's question. "Nope, never." She sighed as he practically gave her a massage."

"Well, that's a shame. You missed out. You're a lucky guy, Bart." He moved onto my wife's back and shoulders.

"Hey is it true that all black guys have big dicks?" My wife asked.

Thompson chuckled for a moment before he responded. "It's mostly true. I guess it's a blessing."

"Well, let's see if you meet the standard." Allison grabbed his crotch with her hand as she gasped. "Wow! You're bigger than big." She sighed.

"Whoa! What are you doing babe?"

"Just feeling him up a bit. Relax honey. Don't get your panties in a bunch."

"You like?" Thompson smiled. He had a big bulge in his swim trunks as my wife continued to stroke him. I was about to step in when Allison stopped me.

"Hey babe, do you mind getting me another margarita from the bar? I'm dying for another drink."

"Well what about Thompson?" I asked.

"What about him? He's giving me a massage as you can see. Just do it."

I hated how Allison was treating me right now, but she left me with no choice. I walked away to the bar as Thompson manhandled my wife.

I decided to get a beer for myself as well. The bartender was a bit slow. It was a little busy at the bar, so I didn't blame him too much. I looked back and was shocked to see

Thompson on top of my wife in the cabana.

What in the world were they doing?

"Sir? That'll be $15." The bartender told me. I gave him a twenty as he went to get the change. I looked back and Thompson and my wife were making out!

What the fuck was going on? They went at it pretty hot and heavy. I became absolutely furious. What was she thinking? She seemed to be enjoying it. At least that's what I saw from the distance. I needed to put a stop to this right away...

Chapter 2

I walked up with the drinks and set them in the table. By the time I had returned, Thompson was back rubbing my wife's back again like nothing had happened.

"Hey babe, I forgot. I booked us a nice couple's spa day at the resort here. I just got a reminder email. We have to go or they'll give our spot away.

"What? You didn't tell me that before."

"Well, I forgot about it. Come on let's go."

"Go. I'll catch up with you later." Thompson said with a smile. What in the world did he mean by that?

"Uh- sure then." My wife said. We packed up our things and left. What a relief. I didn't want her near Thompson for the rest of the trip.

~~~Later that night~~~

I cuddled up against my wife on the bed. She had been a

little distant all day. I reached over and caressed her cheek. I leaned in for a kiss, but she didn't exactly return the favor.

"What do you say we get a little kinky tonight, babe?" I asked her.

"Why?" She asked coldly.

"Because we're on vacation, silly."

"I'm not really in the mood." She said.

"So you were in the mood with Thompson before?"

"What are you talking about?"

"Come on, Allison! I saw you flirting with him. And I saw you kiss him too."

"Well that's because he's a real man!" Allison snapped back at me. She seemed disgusted with me.

"What?"

"I'm tired of your small dick, Bart. It was cute at first, but I need a real man to please me. I haven't had a real orgasm in years. You're so fucking pathetic."

It was a real shock in the system to hear this from my own wife.

"I uh--" I had no words. What was I supposed to say?

"Did you even see Thompson's dick? It was so fucking huge. I want that. I want him." She said. Her eyes lit up when she talked about his manhood. It made me so jealous.

I knew I wasn't exactly the biggest guy, but I had no idea my wife was so unsatisfied with me.

"Well--"

"You know what? I think I'm going to fuck him tonight." Allison said out loud.

"Wait...what?"

"Yeah. You need to be my cuckold or I have no use for you."

Allison stood up and pushed me off the bed.

"Babe, what are you--"

"Shut up, cuck!" She slapped me hard on the face as I tried to get up. She kicked me down again. "Get on the ground!"

Allison was scaring me now. "You're going to serve as my cuck from now on. I had enough of your tiny dick. It's time for a real man to please me."

"I'm not going to be your cuckold!" I shot back at her.

"Yes you are!" She slapped me again. My face must have been so red right now. "Get on your knees, cuckold! You're going to watch as Thompson fucks me tonight." She seemed excited at that thought.

"What? You're fucking crazy!" I spat back at her.

"Do it or I'll get a divorce. I'll take everything you have." She snapped. I knew it would be true. I had a few buddies who got divorced and their wives absolutely fleeced them. I never thought it would happen to Allison and me.

"Please, not that. Don't divorce me."

"Get on your knees and beg me then." She said with devious smile.

I couldn't believe this was happening. I got on my knees before my very own wife. "Please don't divorce me." I pleaded.

"That's right. I'm glad I have your attention now." Allison towered over me with her hands on her hips. I had never felt more ashamed in my life.

"You're doing to service me and Thompson tonight, aren't you?"

"I guess..."

"Good. I was going to sneak out and meet him tonight, but now I think I want you to watch. You're going to watch him fuck my tiny pussy. It's going to feel so good. I'm so wet just thinking about it."

"Please don't--"

"Shut up, stupid cuck. Get ready. I want to see him RIGHT now."

~~~20 minutes later~~~

Allison strolled up with me to Thompson's suite upstairs. It was humiliating accompanying her like this. We were both wearing nothing but the resort robes. We knocked on the door and Thompson answered right away. He wore nothing but a pair of boxer briefs.

"Well hello, beautiful." Thompson said. His eyes lit up as soon as he saw my wife. "And hello to you too, cuck." He chuckled at me. I must have looked so surprised.

"Come in, come in." He beckoned us.

We walked in and Allison ordered me to stand at attention as she made out with Thompson. I felt so pathetic. Who in their right mind would let this happen?

"I can't wait to see your cock." Allison sighed. Her hands rested on his big, broad chest.

"You won't have to wait long. I've been thinking about your pussy all day."

"You have? You're so naughty." My wife laughed. She reached down and caressed his crotch again.

"One thing first. I want to see his stupid tiny dick. I couldn't believe you when you said it was small."

"Are you sure?"

Thompson nodded in response.

I felt so embarrassed when Allison de-robed me in front of Thompson. The soft robe fell to the floor as she pulled it off. My little dick had been exposed.

The two of them laughed their asses off.

"Holy shit! What the fuck is that?!" Thompson pointed at my dick and nearly peed his pants.

I didn't even know what to say in response. I wanted to

come up with a witty comeback, but I had nothing.

"Show him what a real man looks like, baby."

Chapter 3

Thompson dropped his briefs and I was stunned as his big black cock flew out. It was fucking huge. I felt inadequate already.

Allison grabbed onto his giant dick. "This is a real man's cock. Not some stupid clitty that you have."

My cock shriveled up as the two of them taunted me. Normally I was about three inches, but I only measured about two inches right now. Meanwhile, Thompson was literally sporting a 12 inch dick.

"Get on your knees, stupid cuck." My wife ordered.

I fell to my knees. Allison did the same as she grabbed Thompson's dick again. "I wanted to suck on your dick so bad earlier." She moaned.

My wife wrapped her lips around his cock and sucked. "Oh yes! That's a good girl!" Thompson moaned.

He grabbed the back of her head and guided Allison back and

forth. I felt like an idiot kneeling there as another man took advantage of my wife.

"Do you like seeing your wife suck my dick, cuck?" Thompson's booming voice asked me.

"Not particularly." I commented.

"Well, you'll learn to love it." He sneered at me.

Allison began to deep throat his cock. I felt so ashamed.

"Oh god! Your cock is so big!"

"That's right. You're going to feel so much pain when I fuck you."

"Come here, Bart. Hold his cock. See how big it is for yourself." Allison laughed.

I crawled on my hands and knees until I was right next to my wife between his legs. "Hold my dick you fucking pathetic loser."

I reluctantly held his cock in my hand. It felt so big and warm. My wife's saliva was still on his shaft. I could barely hold it in my hands. It felt so powerful like a weapon.

"This dick is going to destroy your wife."

Thompson dick slapped me as he laughed. "Thank me for taking the time to fuck your wife." He said.

"What?"

"Do it you stupid cuck." Allison slapped me upside the head.

"Please fuck my wife, sir." I begged. It must have sounded so pathetic.

"And why would I do that?"

"Because my dick is too small to please her."

"I'm glad you got that right."

"Bow down and kiss my feet."

Allison kicked me from behind and I fell face first to the floor. Thompson's black toes were right in front of me. I planted kisses on them like my life depended on it.

"Alright that's enough. I want to fuck your wife right now. Kneel by the bed."

I crawled right next to the edge of the bed. Meanwhile, Thompson undressed my wife. He pulled the robe off and dumped her on the bed. He grabbed her breast and rolled it around. Next, he sucked in it softly as she moaned.

Allison's fingers reached down and rubbed her wet clit. It was already swollen.

"You want me right now don't you. I can feel it." He asked her.

"Yes! I want your big black cock. Please, Thompson. I need it so bad!"

Thompson chuckled as he slapped my wife's clit a few times before he went in. "Oh god!" Allison moaned.

Thompson was anything but gentle. He punched the first few inches in without going slow. I felt like throwing up from watching another man make love to my wife.

"Oh god!" Allison's fingers dug into his back. She marked him up like a cat. "God fuck me faster. Fuck me faster!" She begged him.

Thompson put his hands on the bed and really went to town on my wife. "You like this?!"

"Yes! I love this!" She moaned.

Thompson moved in and chocked my wife. She gagged and thrashed around. However, I could tell she loved it. He loosened his grip as she moaned. "Fuck! You're so big! I love it!"

I couldn't watch this any longer. I looked down. Thompson caught me gazing away. "Come on cuck! Don't you like watching me fuck your wife?"

"No."

"Shut up. No one cares what you think." Allison laughed at me. Go lick your master's balls as she fucks me."

"Yeah! Lick my sweaty balls!" Thompson laughed at me.

It felt absolutely humiliating. I wanted to die right now instead of licking his balls. I crawled up on the bed perpendicular to him.

"Go on! Get in there!"

The two of them laughed at me as I closed my eyes and licked his balls. They were salty probably from his sweat or piss. I wanted to throw up instantly.

"That was pathetic! Suck on them!"

I had no choice, but to obey. I sucked on his balls like my life depended on it. They were so big like golf balls. It was disgusting.

"That's a good cuck. Now get back up here. I want you to watch as I unload in your wife!"

"Yes! Cum in me baby! Fill me up!"

"Without a condom?"

"We don't need a fucking condom. You're going to clean all of his cum up so I don't get pregnant." Allison laughed at me.

"Are you ready for it?" He growled like an animal.

"Yes! Yes!" My wife moaned. She was screaming at this point.

I watched as Allison used her kegel muscles to strangle his cock. That sent Thompson over the edge as he completely unloaded in my wife.

"Fuck!" He groaned.

My wife screamed as Thompson brought her to another orgasm. Her whole body flayed around. Thompson pulled out of my wife and sprayed her entire stomach and chest. It was humiliating to watch it all.

"Damn that was fucking amazing!" Thompson sighed. He and my

wife were very sweaty from the passionate sex they just had.

"Well, now you have a new task, cuck boy! I'm drenched in his cum. Clean it all up. Start with my pussy."

"What?"

"Do it. Do it now, stupid cuck."

I obeyed like an idiot. Allison had finally broken me. I bowed down and licked up her pussy. It was so swollen. Thompson's cum was still warm.

"Ewww!" He laughed at me. "Eat my fucking cum, you pathetic beta male! I hope you enjoy it!"

Allison pushed my face deeper into her pussy. Thomson's cum smeared all over my facc. All I could taste was the bitter and sour aroma of his jizz. I feared that this would be my life from now on.

"What do you say we take things up a notch?" Allison asked her lover.

"What did you have in mind?"

"Let's fuck at the pool downstairs. Everyone will know that Bart is my cuckold. Let them join in as well. He'll be fucking humiliated."

"I like the sound of that."

"Good. Hey cuck! Clean up! A lot more men are going to fill me up soon!"

"Yes, Allison." I dutifully cleaned out her pussy. I was going to be her cuckold from now on whether I liked it or not.

The Honeymoon Cuckold

Jenni Winters

Chapter 1

"Mmm! How does my pussy taste, honey?" Ceara's fingers caressed the back of my head in the limo.

"Good." I replied.

"Don't you wish you could fuck me right on our honeymoon?"

"Yes. Please. I want to fuck you so bad."

"Shut up cuck. Don't even think about it. I'm going to fuck her pussy instead of you." Luke bellowed from above. His dark lips caressed my wife's neck. His hands reached down and fondled her breasts.

Ceara giggled as another man pleasured her. I couldn't believe my honeymoon was about to start out like this.

"Come on, cuck. Get in there! You're going to be a good pussy eater for me."

My tongue entered deeper into her wet, warm folds. It tasted sweet, but somehow a bitter aftertaste stuck onto my palette.

Ceara and I had just married last week. Things leading up to the wedding were great. However, it was all a deception. The only thing Ceara was after was my money. She could care less about me. She was just a gold digger.

Instead of going on a romantic honeymoon together, she invited her college sweetheart. Luke was a star college basketball player. He was basically superior to me in every single manner. He had looks, charm, and confidence. Every woman wanted to be with him...including my new wife.

Ceara threatened to divorce me if I didn't obey. It was such a humiliating act when she ordered me to beg Luke to come on our honeymoon.

Now, we were on our way to a romantic honeymoon resort in Hawaii. Things looked so good a week ago, but now the world seemed so dim. Ceara had reduced me to a lowly cuckold slave.

I ate her pussy and watched above as she kissed another man. Her nipples became hard as daggers. She moaned into his mouth. Despite all of this, my cock still throbbed.

Ceara was the hottest girl in the entire world. She modeled professionally on occasion and turned heads at all of the parties we attended. I had no idea she was such a cruel mistress.

Luke bent down and sucked on her nipples hard. She moaned softly. "Oh yes, Luke! That feels so amazing!"

"Loser cuck, don't you just love it when I suck on your wife's nipples?"

I was at a complete loss for words. "Hey, Henry. He asked you a fucking question." My wife slapped me on the face. It stung for a brief moment, but the pain really struck my heart.

"Uh yes. I uh like it..." I replied in defeat.

"Yes, what? We went over this already."

"Yes Master. I like it when you suck on her nipples."

The two of them giggled above. It must have looked completely hilarious towering over me in the car. Even our driver had trouble holding back his laughter.

"Mmm I can't wait to feel your dick baby. Just like old times, right?" My new wife caressed her bull's crotch. The outline of his dick looked massive.

"You used to love it so much." He whispered.

"I've never forgotten. Henry's dick is just too small." Her foot caressed my crotch. "He doesn't satisfy me like you do."

"No one ever will." Luke said with confidence.

His large paws caressed every inch of my wife's body. "I can't wait to fuck her and make you watch." Luke said to my face. His hot and stinky breath filled my nostrils.

"Make him beg you to fuck me, babe." Ceara suggested.

Luke practically wet himself laughing. "That's a great idca. Why don't you beg me to fuck your wife on your honeymoon."

I swallowed my pride (or whatever was left of it) and obeyed Luke's order. I had learned that he was the superior man.

I was just here to serve him and Ceara.

"Please fuck my wife." I said in a meek voice. It must have sounded quite pathetic.

"You call that begging? That's fucking pathetic." Luke spat in my face. His saliva hit me directly in the eye. I flinched in response.

Ceara laughed. "That was soooo funny!" She gathered spit and shot one directly onto my nose. "He makes a great human spittoon."

"Beg me with some emotion this time." Luke ordered. His fingers squeezed my wife's breasts.

"Please fuck her my Master. My dick is too small to please her. Please, I beg you!" The last of my pride escaped my lips. I was just a shell of my former self.

"Much better. I think I will. I'll rock her fucking world." He said.

The two of them continued to kiss as I knelt on the floor

of the limo. It was completely awkward to me. My cock twitched in my pants.

Luke looked down at me again. "What are you staring at?"

"Uh nothing, Master." I looked down at their feet.

"You see something you like?" Ceara laughed. "Come lick our shoes clean."

She snapped her fingers as I bowed down like a dog and cleaned the dirt from the soles of their shoes. Ceara wore a pair of sexy black plumps and Luke wore a pair of brown loafers.

The two of them continued to make out as I ate dirt. I guess it was fitting. A dirt bag eating dirt...

Soon enough our ride came to an end. "Alright sir and miss, we're at the resort. That'll be $150 for the ride."

"Pay the nice man, cuck." Ceara ordered me. She and Luke left the car as I fumbled for my wallet. The guy looked at me with such pity. Little did he know things were just heating up for the weekend.

Chapter 2

"Alright let's go check in." Luke said.

"Hold on a second." Ceara dug into her bag and pulled out a dog collar and leash. "On your knees, cuckboy!"

She pointed to the ground in front of her. I obeyed and looked down in utter defeat. "You're going to be our good little dog."

She put the collar and leash around my neck. Luke couldn't hold in his laughter. "Good god! That's fucking pathetic! I hope they don't charge us for a pet fee!" He taunted me.

"Alright, now we're ready to go."

Ceara held tightly onto the leash. I crawled on my hands and knees like a pet dog. It was pathetic. We were staying at an adult nudist resort, so people were usually a little kinkier. However, we still got plenty of stares.

I already saw a few people pointing and laughing at me. I had a feeling this was only the beginning. Ceara and I had booked this resort months in advance for the entire week. It was going to be a long honeymoon.

We quickly made it to the front desk and checked in. The receptionist showed us up to our room. It was only a one bedroom suite. Ceara and Luke would of course be sleeping together on top. They "graciously" allowed me to sleep on the floor beneath their feet.

"What do you say we go to the pool for a bit. We'll have a little fun before starting the fireworks." Luke said. He brought Ceara in close. Her breasts pushed up against his broad chest.

Even I had to admit that Luke was a really handsome and built jock. He was dumb as rocks, but still women liked that I guess.

The two lovebirds stripped each other down. They looked ready to pounce on each other.

"Mmm do we have to? I want you so bad right now." Ceara pelted his neck with kisses. I watched closely as I felt a pang of jealously. I wanted to have my wife so bad on our honeymoon. Unfortunately, it was probably never going to happen.

"Well we could do it outside at the pool. This is an 'adult' resort after all." Luke said with a devious smile.

"Hmm...good idea! Plus I'm sure cuckboy here is dying to watch. Isn't that right?" She shook my collar from side to side.

"Yes Mistress." I replied.

"Good boy. Let's get going then. Want to hold his leash, babe?"

"Sure, why not." Luke replied.

Ceara ordered me to strip down naked. I wanted to protest, but it was futile.

"Is that his dick? It's so fucking tiny!" Luke remarked.

"Yep. That's it."

Ceara bent down and held my four inch dick in her hand. "You're so fucking pathetic. You know that? This wouldn't please anyone."

"Yes, Mistress. I'm very sorry."

She knelt up and held Luke's massive 12 inch black cock. My new wife waved it around my face. "This is a real man's dick." She said proudly.

After that little bit of humiliation, we left for the pool. Luke wasn't quite as gentle handling my collar. He pulled it forward a few times jerking my neck. The tight collar pulled against my skin. I'm sure there would be marks tomorrow morning.

"Good doggy!" A few couples laughed at me from the distance.

"Thanks!" Ceara replied to them.

A few other couples laughed at me. "What in the world is he doing?" An older couple asked.

"Oh don't mind him. He's just our little cuckold." Luke remarked. The older couple didn't even know how to respond.

Ceara and Luke just laughed at me. We finally made it to

the pool. Everyone here was completely naked.

The large Olympic sized infinity pool outlined the outer edge of the lounge. There were cabanas sprinkled around. The sun's ways beamed down on us. It provided a warm blanket around our skin.

"Oh! Yes!" I heard from the distance. Another couple were getting it down and dirty at the pool. There were a few cheers from bystanders watching the sex unfold.

"You hear that, cuck?" Ceara asked me.

"Yes, Mistress?"

"That's the sound of a real women getting pleasured."

We finally found an empty cabana. Unfortunately it was in the middle of the room. Another young couple sat across from us. They looked cute. The girl had short blonde hair and decent sized breasts. The guy was Caucasian and fairly athletic. They watched with much amusement as Luke manhandled me.

"What are you doing to him?" The guy asked.

"Oh he's just our little cuckold. He's going to watch while Luke and I have sex." Ceara replied.

The young couple laughed at my expense. "What does that mean?"

"It means he just services us. He's like a glorified slave." Luke replied.

"Oh my god! That's pathetic! What a loser!" The girl replied.

"Tell me about it." Ceara said.

"I'm Luke, by the way."

"Jason. And this is my wife, Olivia."

"Nice to meet you. This is Ceara."

The couple introduced each other while I knelt at the floor. Ceara began to tell the story of how I came to be.

"So he's really servicing you on your honeymoon?" Olivia asked with much intrigue.

"Yep. We've got him whipped nice and good." My wife answered.

The four superior beings laughed at me.

"If you want...we can let you use him for a while after we have sex." Ceara said.

"You're joking? What would he even do?" Jason asked.

"Watch and see." Luke said.

Ceara ordered me to the edge of the bed in the cabana. Meanwhile, Luke tossed her on as she squealed like a little girl.

Chapter 3

Luke lay on top of my wife as they kissed. His big black dick instantly turned hard. It rubbed against her lower stomach.

"Oh god! Yes! I feel your cock!" She moaned.

Other couples had begun to gather around. Things were heating up. I watched uncomfortably as people whispered around.

"He's just a cuck."

"What the fuck is wrong with that loser?"

I tried to tune out the crowd to focus on my wife and her lover. Luke mounted my wife. His cock pressed softly into her cunt. It looked magnificent. Even I had to admit that I would never be able to please Ceara like that.

"Oh yes! God! I've missed your cock!"

"I missed your pussy too." He replied with a grunt.

Luke punched his cock deeper and deeper into my wife. "Oh!

Go faster! Faster!" She screamed.

People were cheering them on. Luke planted his hands down and fucked her like a jackhammer. Ceara's legs wrapped around his back as her nails dug in. "Oh! Oh! Oh god!"

My little cock twitched in response.

"You like watching me fuck your wife?"

"Yes, Master. I like watching it."

The crowd laughed at me.

"Pathetic cuck!" Someone jeered at me.

Luke continued to focus his attention on my wife. They made out while he continued to ravage her pussy. Her white juice had already coated his big black cock. It was a magnificent scene to behold.

"Come here, cuck. Let me see that pathetic dick of yours." Ceara tugged on my dog leash. I crawled forward next to her on the bed.

She grabbed my dick by the head and squeezed down. "You call this a fucking dick?"

"No it's too pathetic." I replied.

"You're goddamn right!" She spat in my face to the crowd's amusement.

Olivia and Jason looked at me with such disgust. I couldn't believe this was happening. I just wanted to curl up into a ball and die.

"You're not a real man. A real man is fucking me right now. You're just a loser cuck!"

"Yes, Mistress. I know."

Ceara spat in my face again. She smeared it all over with her hand. "Watch as he fucks me, cuckboy!"

The crowd continued to laugh at my expense. It was like they fed off on my humiliation.

Luke pulled out of my wife and turned her on her knees. "I want to see that fine ass as I fuck you." He whispered seductively into her ears.

"Oh yes! Please fuck me!" She begged him. It was so weird hearing my wife beg for another man's cock.

Luke positioned his cock back into my wife and fucked her in doggy. The sounds of his big dick fucking her wet pussy drove me insane. I couldn't explain it, but my cock throbbed. It was so hot.

"Oh!" Ceara moaned into my face. I could see the lust she had for his giant cock. Mine was a pea shooter in comparison.

"Come here cuck! I want you to lick my balls while I fuck your wife!"

"What?"

"I said come HERE!" Luke's deep voice echoed through my eyes. He struck fear into my heart. I didn't dare disobey him at this point.

I crawled onto the bed and knelt down. I stared at his big black balls. They swing back and forth in rhythm like a pendulum.

"Suck on my balls, stupid cuck!"

Reluctantly, I opened my mouth and sucked on his balls. I tasted old piss and sweat. It was utterly disgusting. I wanted to throw up.

"How do my man's balls taste, cuck?" Ceara teased me.

"Ugh!" I groaned. Everyone laughed at me. I even heard a few cameras snapping in the audience. I would never be able to live this moment down.

I was close enough to the action to see Luke's massive cock destroy my new wife's pussy. "Oh god! You're a fucking real man!" She screamed.

Her cunt was swollen and pink to the touch. Her walls stretched out far to take his black cock. I groaned and continued to suck on his balls. All I wanted was for the humiliation to end. My tongue caressed both balls.

"Ugh! Oh yes!" Luke moaned from above.

Ceara grabbed the leash again and thrashed it around. The collar slid from side to side around my neck and burned my skin.

"Argh!" I groaned out in pain. That only provided oil to the fire. Ceara loved to see me in pain.

"I'm ready for your cum, baby. Give it to me now!"

"Yeah? You want it?"

"Yes! Cum in me! Cum for me!" Her sultry voice beckoned Luke closer and closer to orgasm. I knew it wouldn't be long until be spilled his entire load on her.

"Fuck yeah! I love your cunt!"

Luke grabbed my wife's waist and rammed his cock deep down her pussy. He grunted one last time and spilled his filth. I felt his balls tighten up in my mouth. He completely unloaded. His balls drained out of my mouth into my wife's pussy.

"Oh god! Yes!" Ceara moaned.

The entire crowd oohed and ahed. It was absolutely humiliating.

"God! That felt so good!" My wife groaned.

Luke pulled out as the cum dripped from her pussy like a waterfall. It was everywhere.

"Clean it up! Clean it up! Clean it up!" The crowd chanted.

Luke laughed as he grabbed me by the back of the neck and forced me down to her pussy. "Clean it stupid cuck!"

"Yeah clean it fucker!" Ceara added on. It was like rubbing salt on the wound.

I closed my eyes and sucked on her pussy. I tasted Luke's superior seed. It was salty, bitter, and disgusting. I had never had anything so gross in my mouth.

"Ugh! Oh god!" I groaned. I fought for dear life to resist throwing up.

After a few minutes, Luke let me back up. I fell on my back as the crowd laughed. Eventually everyone dispersed. The fun action was gone. They were off to see another show.

Jason and Olivia stayed behind in complete awe.

"Oh my god! That was so hot!" Olivia squealed.

"If you want, we can lend you our cuck for the night. He basically does whatever you want." Ceara said. Lend me to another couple? It was my worst fear...

"You're joking?" Jason said completely surprised.

"Nah take him for a spin. You'll have so much fun." Luke said.

Ceara handed the young couple my collar. Olivia took it. Things were about to get even worse for me...

About The Author

Jenni began writing erotica as a way to channel her biggest fantasies. Now, she loves spreading her dirty stories across the web so others can enjoy!

If you LOVE wife watching, cuckolding, cheating wives, and BIG BLACK BULLS, you've come to the right place. Most of Jenni's cuckold stories are based on personal experience, stories of friends, or just her dirty mind in action.

Printed in France by Amazon
Brétigny-sur-Orge, FR